FAT
WOMAN

FAT
WOMAN

LEON ROOKE

Alfred A. Knopf   New York   1981

THIS IS A BORZOI BOOK
PUBLISHED BY ALFRED A. KNOPF, INC.

Library of Congress Cataloging in Publication Data
Rooke, Leon. Fat woman.
I. Title.
PS3568.O6F37 1981   813'.54   80-21893
ISBN 0-394-51642-7

Manufactured in the United States of America
First American Edition

For John Metcalf

O fat white woman whom nobody loves,
Why do you walk through the fields in gloves,
When the grass is soft as the breast of doves
  And shivering-sweet to the touch?
O why do you walk through the fields in gloves . . .

FRANCES CORNFORD

FAT
WOMAN

What she sees as she slows to turn Edward's truck into the driveway is a complete stranger in bulky overalls perched up there on a ladder and sticking his head through her bedroom window for no reason on God's green earth known to her. Her heart—not reliable, anyhow—quickens, and for a second she fears it may stop altogether. One day it will, sure enough. You can't expect a thing to go on pulling what it isn't meant in the first place to be hitched up to. That's what Edward is always telling her, and she knows no better authority than Edward. *Now don't poke out your lips till they get stepped on, you know I wasn't criticizing. Whatever I tell you is for your own good.*

She makes the turn too soon and a front tire bolts up over the curb, setting off a drone somewhere under the hood, while behind her there comes a clang and thump from all the broken-down contraptions Edward has ever found in ditch, field, or back alley, and thrown inside for the salvage only he can find in them. *Half a day for screw or rusty nail, but worth the effort, Ella Mae.* Now she sees a blur of denim through tree and hedge and lets escape a cry of small satisfaction. "I wasn't dreaming," she murmurs. "A Peeping Tom right here in broad daylight and what is he going to do to me when I tell him to his face what a sorry no-account creature he is for scaring the daylights out of me?" She hears the nasty switch of hedge against the truck side and once again impulsively swerves, this time sending canned goods and a box of Zesta crackers—cheaper than Ann Page and every bit as crispy— flying under her feet from grocery bags on their own seat beside her. Whimpering, she pumps at the floorboard pedals, gets tangled where the canned goods roll, and manages one hurried prayer to her Savior: *Take me, Lord, if you want to, but don't let me put a single scratch on Edward's Ford.* The garage door looms ahead and she gasps, pumping fitfully at the brake as front tires flounder dizzily through driveway ruts, all but wrenching the steering wheel from her grasp. The truck goes on bucking and coughing and sputtering, as if it would have her learn now and forever that the one thing it has is a mind of its own. With a shriek she yanks at the emergency brake, certain as she does so that it will come loose in her hand the way it never does with Edward, and already throwing a protective arm across her face against that moment when his truck will crash like a battering ram through the door and into all the powerful secrets he has in there.

I t comes to her a few seconds later that the truck is no longer moving, that the garage door is intact. She has been spared this fresh indignity. God will punish her, there is never a time when she does not believe this, but He will have to think up something better now than wreck and ruination in her own front yard. Flushed and dizzy, she sits with closed eyes, drinking in air by the mouthful and endeavoring to will back breath and dignity—if not one then the other and lucky to get both. The Zesta box is smashed and her ankle throbs where tomato cans have shot at her and found bone. Edward is right in this as in all matters: she is too excitable, too daydreamy, she has too much air between her ears ever to be allowed to go driving on city streets by herself. *A person your size and substance can't go running about like no spring chicken, Ella Mae. You'd best stay home and faint and swoon with me here to look after you, with me here to provide lock and key.*

She opens her eyes and gradually becomes aware that the brake handle is still tight in her hand. She pushes this in slowly, click by click, now kicking the Zesta box aside, saying to herself in a good clear voice, "I knew when I bought that box that it wasn't a thing I had any need for."

The sound of her own voice is reassuring, and although there is no joy in her just now, she laughs. One loaf of light bread—Sweet Breeze, it is called, the same bread her mama sent her to the store for when she was little—has burst open and fanned out over the floorboard, slice upon slice. What she can reach she quickly scoops up and stuffs into her mouth, swallowing almost without chewing, a packed wad of dough that hurts as it slides down. Her eyes moisten but she thinks: *I feel better now. I'm punished. Ella Mae, darling, you can carry on.*

But she makes no move yet to escape the confines of Edward's Ford. That odd droning noise—like something alive and forlorn, like something lost that knows it will never be found—continues under the hood, and it is a sound that carries her mind back miles and miles, to another day, another time. *The pups,* she thinks, *the puppy dogs and kittens which my daddy would drop alive and kicking into a gunnysack, which he'd then throw into the creek near our house, that is what I'm reminded of.* The sight is fresh in her mind as yesterday, that bagful of sorrowful, whiny, wriggling shapes. The current sweeping them away as if they were nothing more than a bag of sticks, while her daddy stood by without remorse or compunction, complaining with every breath of more mouths than solitary man could feed. *If their bitch mama has got to do what she does, I reckon as how I've got to do what I'm doing now. So hush your sniveling, child, unless you want me to throw you in with them.*

"I will never forgive you, Daddy," she now remarks, "your cruelty to those innocent creatures of God."

Nor can she forgive herself. She does not know why there should be a strange man in overalls at her bedroom window, but she knows—Ella Mae thinks she does—why this near-accident has happened. It has nothing to do with ladders propped against her house. It has happened because once again she has given in to her weakness, she has let Satan tempt her. She has let Lucifer plant his flag, she has enjoyed herself, marching right along to his music. God saw everything. And despite what her church preached and what folks said her Bible proved, it often seemed to her that there was very little He forgave. As clearly as the drowning animals she saw a moment ago, she could now see God shaking His finger at her across swirling clouds, saying *Ella Mae Hopkins, you have been out feeding your face when you should have been at home washing Edward's clothes and cleaning his house and seeing to your boys. You're a pig, Ella Mae.*

Rounding the corner of the house, Ella Mae receives another shock. For up there on a ladder, looking cute as can be with his T-square dangling from his belt and a pencil clamped between his teeth, is her Edward. It stuns her to think that even momentarily she could have mistaken for someone common as a Peeping Tom this man she has slept with, had children by, lived with in holy matrimony for twenty-seven years. She squints up at him and a flash of sun stabs her smack in the eyes. What she sees, or halfway sees, is the Son of God walking the blue water of the sky, both arms raised as if to signal his return. *I am not ready,* she groans, and the confession is humiliating. She has an urge to run into the house, scramble under the bed, and hide. She blinks, shading her eyes, though this helps not at all, as his scowling Eminence penetrates clear on through her fingers. *I am not ready,* she hears herself say, *I thought I told you that!* The voice in her head is rude, petulant as a child's, and it horrifies her that anyone, much less Ella Mae Hopkins, should dare speak so to God's only Son. As a child she had this game. She would close her eyes and at the count of ten open them, crying, *I'm coming, ready or not!* She would search every nook and cranny and when at last she'd given up, Jesus would step out whistling from behind some far-off tree or barn and she would run to him and he would sweep her up into his arms.

"Oh, Lord," she hears herself moaning now, "it's the truth, I was ready then."

Now that I've got Edward, she means. *Now that I've got my sweet Edward, I can't bear to part from earth.*

"You got troubles, Ella Mae? You having one of your spells?"

The blue sky closes and it is only Edward talking to her from up there, arms flapping out from his sides with no more meaning than chicken wings.

"Don't faint on me, Ella Mae. I'd sooner walk on hot coals in my birthday suit as have to pick you up."

It is only Edward up there, grinning ear to ear, running on with his usual nonsense. Standing straight up on the ladder's narrow step, with only his natural kinship with a monkey to keep him from landing in her rosebushes and breaking open his head.

"How come you're home?" she asks. "You get yourself fired?"

"They wouldn't fire me," he hollers. "I'm the only soul down at the yard does any work! They'd fold up like a twenty-cent accordion, they didn't have me to rely on."

She shoots him a tender look, having heard this for years and now believing it without question.

"Glad to see you made it home safe and sound," he adds. "Truck act up on you any?"

She tells him no. No, it behaved good as a baby.

She remains rooted just wide of the corner of the house, separated from him and her front door by a scant twenty yards, space she has neither the strength nor the will to cross. Her skin feels uncomfortably moist. Dead sweat, that is how she thinks of it. All morning long this sweat has disgusted her with its oily beads that raise wet patches under her arms, that roll down her backside and thighs and send heat pouring into her shoes. The awful sweat has dried now in the faint wind, sending a flurry of cold shivers over her as she watches Edward—*Someone walking over your grave* is what her mama would say.

"How's the sore finger?" she hears him ask. And a cackle erupts, sounding like a rooster with its crowing run down, though it is only Edward having his fun with her. She does not answer.

What she wants most in the world is to sit down and take the weight off her legs. To sit and take stock of where she's got herself to this morning. But she would not sit down with Edward watching, and in any case she could not sit out here in the front yard because Edward has removed her lawn chair. He has put it inside the garage with all the other gear he says needs fixing. *I will get to it soon, no need to worry, then you can sit to your heart's content and report back to me all the juicy bits going on in the neighborhood.*

This was six weeks ago, and not a hand lifted in that direction since. No, he can climb ladders and stand there flapping his arms, taunting her about sore fingers, but he can't find the time to put new webbing on her chair. He has got a mess of weathered boards strewn over her yard, next to his sawhorse and his million dollars' worth of power tools, and he has made a wreck of her rosebushes getting his ladder put up. She is burning with curiosity over this job he's working on at her window, and she aches to ask him what in Tom Fool's name he thinks he's doing. But it is best not to inquire. *When the job is done,* he would tell her, *that will be time enough for you to know.*

"If I had me a finger like that," he says, "I'd sell it to a museum! People would pay good money to see it."

This remark angers her, though she says nothing. She has gone shopping and gorged herself on ice cream and driven his Ford through city streets with a kitchen mitten on her right hand, and she will not take that mitten off now so she can hear him tell her again that the finger has gone gangrenous, that soon its poison is apt to leak in and short-circuit her whole system. She has put up with pain, put up with it all her natural life, and she reckons she can put up with this ugly swollen finger.

"I put up with *you!*" she shouts at him, suddenly laughing. "I reckon I can put up with this finger!"

He ogles her, his head made scrawny and sinister by the strong light behind him. Then he picks up his cigarette from the windowsill and takes a deep drag, his head pitched back in such a way that he looks exactly like a baby bird stretching its long neck for worm or water.

"I don't have all day to waste on you," she tells him. But she makes no move as yet to leave, and for an answer Edward just snickers. Her shoes are on fire, her legs wobbly, and a trickle of blood has run down her ankle where a tomato can or loose metal in Edward's truck has reached out and stabbed her. Her skin has always been delicate, too white and too soft and too easily bruised. "Almost a bleeder," she murmurs, having in mind that man she recently read about in *The National Enquirer*. The poor thing had lost his card reading I AM A BLEEDER when his pocket was picked on a busy downtown street in Toledo, Ohio, and before he could replace it, he'd been beaten up in New York, New York, and left to bleed to death in a hospital waiting room where the staff was on a slowdown for higher wages. What puzzled her about that story was why an afflicted person like a bleeder felt he had to jitterbug around the world so much, and why it was that otherwise sensible people would choose to live in a big zoo of a city in the first place. She could thank her lucky stars she and Edward and their two boys had been spared that sad fate.

The chills have passed and she feels all hot and perspiry once more. She stands fanning her face with her dress, hating this body. Her flesh has a mind of its own and is as moody as an orphaned child or hand-me-down wife. Edward stops snickering long enough to scoot down the ladder, pick up one of his sawed-off boards, and scoot back up again.

If she has one bone to pick with her Edward, it is this retarded snickering habit of his.

"I'm all worn out," she moans, summoning up her reserves and at last heading for the front door. "The store was pack-jammed and it took me forever to find what I needed."

Edward pulls a nail from the row of nails stuck in his mouth like extra teeth, and she pauses on the doorstep to hear his response to this simple declaration.

"Oh, I bet you got what you needed!" he sings. "I'd wager my last dollar on that!"

This is his way of telling her that he knows she has stopped off someplace for a treat, but that it is against his good nature to hold her accountable for what she cannot help—so she laughs along with him. It pleases her, as she looks past him into the blue vacant sky, to remind herself how fortunate she is to have latched on to a good-humored man, to one who could see the fun in life without having to be beat over the head.

She takes a final gander at the window before passing into the house. "Are you winterizing, Edward?" she asks, quite certain she is sounding every bit a fool.

"Doing nothing much," he calmly replies. "You don't need pay me no never-mind."

In three quick strokes of his hammer, he nails up the first wide board.

Inside, she presses her backside against the door, drawing deep breaths, surveying with affection the warm interior of this house God and Edward have provided for her. *Home safe,* she thinks, *and no bones broken.* Wondering why it is that braving Edward's teasing is like having a buzz saw tear at her insides. He's the most secretive man alive, she reflects, and recalls with no little pain that ten years went by in their married life before she pried out of him his middle name. Henry, a fine old-fashioned name, hardly one that people would laugh at to hear. But what a worry that new name had been to her, fearing their marriage was not legal and binding since nowhere on the certificate was there mention of any *Henry* she was wedded up with. To this day, on paper it was plain Edward Hopkins who had won her hand and consummated between sheet and bedpost this union otherwise made in heaven. *Naive,* he had said she was, *to be worrying your head about what tag I have. You think this Edward Hopkins is going to sweep down on a white horse and run off with you? You think yours truly, Edward* Henry *Hopkins, wouldn't punch that wife-stealer in the nose and grab you out of the saddle? Naive ain't the half of it, Ella Mae. You're so innocent you think skunk don't stink nor Tom Cat prowl.*

She places the few groceries she has brought in on the cutting board by the sink, and stops to wash her hands, to press a cool damp cloth against her neck and face and arms. I ought to get out of this terrible dress, she tells herself, for it is sticking to her skin like glue. But she lacks the energy just now. She has the theory, not repeated to anyone, that these tight dresses cut off the normal flow of blood—which is why she gets dizzy sometimes—but it would break her heart to let out the seams and expand the gussets and enlarge the waistbands of these drip-dries yet another time. If there were any justice in the world she'd be able to go to the store and buy herself a dress sizable enough to fit in the first place.

By craning her neck and standing on a footstool, she can just see through the sink window to the side of the house and Edward, from the knees down, on the ladder. To her way of thinking, Edward on a ladder is as good as any circus man. That had been one of his specialties back as way-far as their courting days, one of his means of amusing her and himself too, for nothing bored Edward so much as a simple straight-out walk to a place.

No, he wasn't one for getting to anyplace fast. He had to chase around, hide behind trees and jump ditches, throw rocks at tin cans, Pepsi bottles, or cats, or streak across fields as if ghosts were after him. He was such a treasure, that man. Stopping and splashing sticks into mudholes, disappearing into thickets where his invisible voice would shout out *You're nice, Ella Mae* or *Where you going, Hoecake?* or *Hey, gal, who's your boyfriend?* And at some point before these walks were over, when you had finally decided that this time you had escaped, he had to sneak up behind you and give a loud sudden *Boo!* that made your skin leap off its bones. He couldn't pass a bush without swatting it or an anthill without kicking it, and if he ever stopped his foolishness long enough to actually touch you, well, your knees would go limp and you'd stroll the rest of the way home in a daze. But these antics were nothing compared to his love for ladders. Whenever he saw one leaning against house or barn, he went truly crazy, and even when he had no idea who lived at a place, even if they were sorry and no-account and not worth spitting at, he'd shout *Ya-hoo!* like an Indian and race off at full speed to climb the rungs to their full height without once making use of his hands. At the top, standing up straight with nothing between himself and broken limbs but thin air, he'd twist around with a big grin, and wave. *Learned it in the Navy,* he'd smirk, being rightly proud.

The biggest cut-up you ever saw, she now thinks, delighted with the memory, seeing him all the way back there in time, crowing at her from the rooftops of so many houses and tumbledown barns. *A monkey got nothing on me, Ella Mae!*

Yet a deep and serious man even then, which, thank the Lord, she had the good sense to realize.

She draws a pan of hot water and sinks into a chair to

bathe her swollen feet. Water sloshes onto the linoleum floor. The water is going to leave spots in her wax if she lets it stand, and she will, for she has not the strength just now to move. That is as good as any other reason to cry, and she does. It has been that way of late: tears overtaking her like a runaway bull, tears that heave up out of her depths to leave her choking with exhaustion. She removes at long last the potholder mitten from her hand. But she will not look at the offending finger. She will put it and her pain out of her mind. She will think of nothing.

From time to time over the next half-hour, Ella Mae was aware of Edward's hammer beating against the side of the house, of the intermittent whine of his drill or saw. She told herself not to think about it. Edward was a good handyman, always up to something. There wasn't any point, Edward said, in spending hard-earned money on store-bought goods when he could do a job himself. He'd put in her kitchen counter and her cabinets, he'd laid the new linoleum and built the table she was sitting at. Nobody could say he was shiftless in his chores, like some people she could name. There were times when she felt a little sorry for Edward, believing as she did that a man of his merits deserved more of the world than what had come to him. Not, mind you, that anyone ever heard him complain. To look at Edward, a person would swear he was the most contented creature alive, and of course everyone marveled at his talent with his hands, just as they secretly envied the easygoing nature that won him so many friends down at the yard. She didn't know how many girls she'd grown up with—grown women now—who had wished aloud in her company that they'd had the luck or good sense to snatch him up. *He don't drink, he don't cuss, he don't run around. Ella Mae, you can count your blessings the day you landed him.*

But lately she found herself wondering sometimes, from the way she'd catch him eyeing her or one of the boys, whether they were not all a yoke around his neck. Whether she and the boys were not holding him back. He ought, for one thing, to be running the yard. A man like Edward, who people naturally looked up to because they could see he had pride *and* brains, a real go-getter, ought to have a regular position he could count on and maybe his name on a brass plate on a big desk. Yes, it seemed to her that Edward was unhappy, though it cut her to the heart to admit it and Edward would be the last one ever to show it. She wondered if this didn't come from his having been a Navy man; after sailing the ocean blue and seeing so many foreign countries and the curious ways people had of living in them, could he ever be truly happy in this place he'd been born and raised? He had that dreamy look in his eyes. Always had, though now more and more. You could be sitting at the table talking to him and most times he wouldn't hear a word you said. *Huh? What was that, Ella Mae?* Not that he was exactly the talkative kind, you couldn't say that of him even when he was in the best of moods. Even his own mama had admitted to that much, and she had thought the sun rose and set on her Edward: *He's a dark bird, my Edward is. But be thankful for your blessings, child. If they ain't grabbing at you in one need, they're bossing you around in another.*

Well, Edward wasn't the grabbing kind, nor the bossing either. She could thank her beans for that.

And of course lately, these last few years, there had

been less and less grabbing until now he hardly grabbed at all.

Oh, he could pretend he liked a large woman, a woman with size, he could even say it now and again, but deep-down she knew he'd given up hoping to find ever again what he'd once found in her.

She wished she had her own mama alive today to talk to her about Edward.

She was thinking of her mama and trying to hold back her tears when the screen door slammed and Edward stumbled in, a strain on his face, holding three grocery bags high in his arms. "Forgot, hope nothing ain't spoiled," he wheezed, and stood by panting, asking where she wanted her bags put. Before she could answer, he'd pushed her potted plants aside and shoved them onto the counter. "Woo!" he exclaimed, wiping his brow, "I've carried lead, iron, steel, and a passel of worries, but that's the heaviest load I *ever* carried!"

Well, you've never carried me, she thought to say, but didn't.

"I was sitting here thinking of Mama in her grave," she said. "Else I would have reminded you."

He nodded absentmindedly, sniffing over the tops of the bags.

Her Edward was every inch a gentleman. He never let her bring in groceries or carry out garbage, so long as he could help it. Thinking this, she smiled guiltily up at him, lifting the plate of cookies he'd found her munching on. "You want some?"

He shook his head. She could see him looking at her ugly hurt finger out of the corners of his eyes, and quickly she hid it between her legs. His eyes dropped down to her feet there in the pan of water gone ice cold. He stood undecided, fidgeting, something on his mind. "Spots on that there linoleum," he finally said. Then tugging at the crotch in his overalls, saying, "Well, if you're done with me."

"I'm done. You can go on with your hammering, if you've a mind to."

He turned on his heels and went back outside. After a while she heard him pounding again. She got up and padded in her wet feet to where the cookies were stored, counting out three more oatmeals for herself. Disgusted, she put two of them back. But before the lid was closed she got them out again. She reckoned God would forgive her for taking one or two extra. *I need them,* she thought. *I need them for my nerves.*

On her side, too, was the fact that she'd had a poor night's rest. A whole train of them, stretching back weeks and weeks. She had no trouble accounting for this. For some time now she'd had the unmistakable feeling, more like a shadow hanging over than any specific something she could put her finger on, of an impending horror. Of terrible news soon to come her way. *Her* way, for she did not believe it included Edward or the boys directly. Good works could not erase this foreboding. She could work her fingers to the bone and still it hovered there. Although there had been days when she thought this was foolishness, thought her fear was vanity and wanting more than God saw fit to give her, her sense of the terrible threat abided. Another person, more sensible, would long ago have got on the phone to Preacher Eelbone. Would have said, at a minimum, *Preacher, will you pray for me?* Some part of her found this practice repugnant. It was the Christian thing to do, certainly, but it struck her as the height of impudence to ask the Lord's servant to intercede for someone so small in God's plans as Ella Mae Hopkins. And God too, she feared, not to take away from His omnipotence and compassion, would have no choice but to glare down through the open sky and say for Edward and the whole town to hear, *Gluttony, thy name is Ella Mae!*

The front door slammed. She shoved the cookie tin away in time, as Edward strolled past the kitchen door carrying a piece of plywood big as a barn. He went on upstairs with it.

Another mystery, but never you mind, she told herself. If there was one thing she was certain of, it was that Edward always knew and had good reasons for whatever he was doing. Not poky and hound-dog, like some people. No, he got right down to his chosen tasks, you wouldn't find him hem-hawing around all day. The way she was doing herself today, to tell the truth. The house was a mess, it was crying for a good cleaning up. Edward didn't seem to mind filth, but she didn't approve of children coming home from school and finding the place looking like a cyclone had hit it. If you raised sons in a pigsty, boys who noticed things the way her two did, well, when they married they'd find themselves a slatternly wife who'd give them what they were used to. And she wouldn't be able to stand that.

She rinsed her coffee cup, ate the last few crumbs off her saucer, and rinsed that. She set out her lard so it would be at room temperature when she got around to making her biscuits. She got three pounds of hamburger out of the deep freeze and four jars of canned goods—okra and corn and sweet peas and stewed tomatoes—from the pantry. Well, she kept her menfolk's stomachs full, no one could fault her on that account. Although she knew well enough what

Edward would say: *It ain't* my *stomach, Ella Mae, that I'm worrying about.*

She got out her Eureka and spent the best part of the hour vacuuming the living room and what they called the den, which is where Edward had the old TV he'd found and was taking apart and where the boys did their homework when she could keep them still long enough to do it. The TV had a tinted blue screen, which he meant to use as a tabletop, the wiring would come in handy, and the wooden cabinet was full of good mahogany veneer, which he expected to find a use for. He would, she didn't doubt that. You couldn't say about Edward that he lacked ideas. There was no need to throw away the tubes either, because the boys could have some fun with them. In his growing-up days, he had told them, a boy had nothing to do but kick tin cans and blow off a thumb playing with firecrackers—"So you can be thankful I'm giving you these." The boys hadn't seen much sense in it but they had taken them, knowing, she reckoned, that they'd get a whupping if they didn't. The boys knew which side of their bread was buttered, all right; you wouldn't find them giving any sass to their daddy. They looked up to him, too. In their eyes nobody measured up to Edward. Blessed be the Lord, she thought, putting away the vacuum, for I'd sooner shoot myself than raise a sorry child.

Sunlight blazed through the living room picture window wide enough for a person to sleep on. Her mama used to tell her that was the way God got places, by riding beams of sunlight wherever it was that folks needed Him. "Mama," she'd say, "ain't it about high time He called on you?" And her mama would wag her finger and say she guessed He had been busy lately. "Up to His neck in trouble," her heathen daddy would say, "like always."

The sun here at the window had faded the sofa cover.

She laughed at herself, thinking that the sofa had been sitting here bleached all winter long and she had just noticed it. Well, it was only a throw cover, never mind. She rubbed an arm against her brow, feeling sweaty. It comes from standing in a hot spot, she told herself, when I ought to know better. All the same, she felt a familiar wave of sleepiness and momentarily closed her eyes.

She could steal upstairs and take one of her catnaps and likely as not Edward would never be the wiser. Though far as that went, there seemed precious little he didn't soon learn about. Eyes in the back of his head, her mama would say.

She saw him down on his knees in the yard, taking a measurement on his mystery boards, his head cocked to one side like a chicken's. She had to laugh, seeing him that way, knowing how it would hurt him should she ever say such a thing to his face. Him, with his insides sensitive as an oyster's. She tapped on the window and waved, but he went right on working. He'd work right through his supper if she let him. He was hooked up to a Sear's DieHard battery, her Edward was, and had energy enough for the two of them. She reckoned that's why it made him so mad sometimes to see her always looking so petered out. Of course, being nothing but skin and bones, he had nothing to slow him down.

She yawned, and quickly slapped a hand over it.

Upstairs, she set the clock alarm for 2:45, not wanting the boys to come home from school and find her sprawled out in bed like an alcoholic. There was no alcoholic in this house, thank the Lord for that. The plywood Edward had brought up was leaning against the wall outside the bedroom door, and as she went by she wondered to herself what on earth Edward was up to. Well, she thought, if I needed to know, I reckon he would have told me. From the bathroom she got a damp washcloth—a trick for keeping cool which she had learned from her mama—and lay down on the bed in her clothes in case she had to jump up quick. She enjoyed these afternoon naps, in fact didn't know how she could manage without them. She'd felt better about stealing the time after reading in *Photoplay* that one half-hour catnapping was worth three or four times that amount in night sleep and was what top models did to keep their poise and beauty when they didn't have a session. She'd made the mistake of showing that article to Edward, who had poked fun, saying that if a half-hour napping did that much then he supposed if she took a three-hour nap she wouldn't need no night sleep at all. Then he'd sat at the kitchen table whistling between his teeth and leafing through her magazine until he came to the full-page ad for Weightlosers Anonymous with its Before and After shot of Bette Wiffle, who had dropped from a size 42 to a size 16 in six short weeks without exercising or dieting and was now having the time of her life in Antigonish, Nova Scotia. "Goes to show you, Ella Mae," he'd said, tapping the page, "it can be done."

She shifted the pillow under her head and stretched the top sheet up to her chin. She closed her eyes and sucked in a good clean breath, then lay very still, setting her mind free to roam where it would.

The first time she went out with Edward on a proper date, after he had asked would she be his girl and she had said she would, he told her he didn't mind her size. *More for me,* he said. *These arms going to hold nothing but woman from here on out.*

I had nice feet and nice hands and my wrists and

ankles were wonderfully thin. I walked with my toes pointed straight in front, and I learned to hold my head up high. I had my mama's hair.

Edward liked running his hands through my hair. My hair was fine like Mama's, though not nearly so long. She never cut hers, not in all her life. It flowed down to her knees and not one strand ever went gray. I would stand behind her in the rocking chair and plat one length while she platted another, Mama holding it and twisting it over her chest, her little fists spinning like a wheel. As mindless about it as could be, like it wasn't hair she was platting but order and harmony she was giving to her life.

Through the day she wore it pinned tight in a bun on her scalp and every night she took it down. She'd fan it and brush it, and the part hard to get at she'd drape over a chair. It was the undertaker finally cut her hair. No need burying this, he said. If this was Taiwan you could sell it, I reckon. Some folks like to keep it, anyhow. Then he passed my mama's hair to my daddy in a yellow bag, which my daddy tried to say he'd forgot, and wouldn't go back for when we left to go home.

My daddy owned a small cracked mirror, which hung by wire on the parlor door, though we didn't call it our parlor as that's where Mama and Poppa slept. Two or three times a week he'd strop his razor cutting edge sharp, and shave in the mustard glass. I wonder what it is about a man's shaving that so draws a child's eyes. Maybe it's taking off the stubble that hides what some would say was their beastly insides. With him done, I could back up across the room, getting smaller and smaller until I was only a fat dot about to disappear. My mama would come in and see me watching myself and she'd say, Now stop scrunching up your face, Ella Mae! Do you think a man will ever want to marry you with you looking like that?

My mama never had a nice bedside table like the one I have, nor a pretty box of nose tissues waiting by on it for whenever she needed one. She'd have had her head cut off before she would be found like me, here dozing in the middle of the day. She didn't have my nice bed. Theirs was an iron frame painted once upon a time and the slats were always falling out. I'd have to crawl under the bed with the daddylonglegs and the dead spiders and flies to put the slats back in place. Many the time I'd be wakened of a dark night from sound sleep by the gunshot sound they made falling out. In the morning my mama would say, Oh that was just your daddy grabbing, go on about your business, child.

Our house was up off the ground on rock posts and in the summer it was wonderfully cool under there. You could crawl under and sit and cool off and in the dark of the lowest parts. You could hide in pits the dogs had dug and never be found.

Sometimes my mama would dip Tube Rose snuff and she'd say, Child, go break off a twig of that lilac bush and bring it here to me. And she'd put the twig in her mouth and work it with her lips in such a way that she could spread the flavor around and keep her teeth clean without once lifting her hands.

I was a scaredycat in my bed at night. I'd wake grinding my teeth and shaking, my throat so dry I couldn't cry out. Mama would come in with a lamp in her hand, the wick turned high and still smoking, Mama's hand cupping the globe to keep out wind. Mama would stroke my face and sink her warmth down, saying, There, there, child, don't you weep no more. Sleep, Ella Mae, sleep, my darling. That's the honey, that's my sweet little girl.

Then I could sleep. I would slumber like a princess, storing up energy to take me through the ripe fine life I was going to have one day.

Ella Mae waked sometime later to find the room in darkness, the washcloth in a hot ball behind her neck, her dress bunched up around her thighs. Her first thought was that she'd gone and slept plumb through the afternoon. If she had, it would be the doghouse for her because Edward would have had a conniption fit trying to deal with the boys, who would be hollering for their dinner. The house, however, was silent. It was eerie too, she thought, and sensed that something funny was going on here. It was dark, all right, but it seemed to her that it was darkness of a different sort, more like she had been cast into some kind of spell. She looked to the window, where not a crack of daylight showed, and to the door which she was certain she had left open. She could barely make out the outline of her own feet, which anyhow had gone numb. Her right arm was sore too from how she'd slept on it, and she had the usual crick in her neck. Edward, bless his heart, was fond of saying that if she ever rolled on him in her sleep he'd wake up smushed like a cockroach, but it seemed to her she was the one who got the worst of sleep. The silence was unnerving and she listened under a strain, squinting to read the clock's indistinct numerals. Not a sound came to her, as if the whole house had been caught under the spell. The devil, she thought, walking about in a pair of his many shoes. She lifted her legs to the floor and sat hunched over, waiting for the blood to drain down into her feet. Then she padded in her stockings out into the hall.

"Edward?" she called. "Are you there?"

Daylight was so bright here she had to close her eyes.

Standing there like that, it came to her that the house was empty, that she was alone, the children not yet home from school, Edward having dropped everything and gone back to the yard.

Her insides were tied up in a knot, wanting food, but she resolved to wait until dinner. She turned back into the bedroom, ignoring Edward's plywood and screws and screwdriver and the fold-up ruler he'd left in the hall. At the bedroom window were Edward's boards, what he called tongue and groove, blocking the familiar view of the front yard, the street, and Eula and Fred Joyner's trailer house across the way. Blocking everything. She pressed her hands against the boards, grunting as she pushed, but they would not budge.

"Is he expecting a hurricane?" she asked aloud.

The room echoed the question back, and she was struck with such a sadness that she dropped back onto the bed and sobbed quietly. She would stay here, she vowed. She would not move or speak to him or even make his dinner. She would do nothing—not do the wash or sweep or pick up after him or take a bath. She wouldn't even eat until he came to her and promised to put her beautiful room back the way it had been.

The night before, Ella Mae had made upwards of sixty oatmeal cookies. Now the tin was empty and she couldn't figure it. Where could they all have gone? She made herself a bologna sandwich and sat down at the kitchen table to puzzle it out, writing with a pencil on one of the grocery bags. She'd packed five each in the boys' lunch boxes and she'd let

them have two or three apiece at breakfast. Edward
hadn't wanted any, he didn't have a sweet tooth anywhere in his mouth. She couldn't believe she'd eaten
more than fifteen herself. So that left maybe thirty unac-
counted for. Well, maybe she'd eaten a few more than
she thought—make that twenty missing cookies. The
same old story, she told herself, getting up to fetch the
warmed-over coffee she could hear boiling on the stove.
You made a batch of cookies and they just up and disappeared as if they had wings. She scooped three full sugars
into her cup and poured in a generous amount of milk,
still mad at Edward. She drank the coffee and finished
off the sandwich, then walked out in the yard, intending
to look at the window from the outside. But she saw Eula
Joyner come to her door and check the mailbox, and she
ducked back inside before Eula got a chance to call to
her. That woman could talk the ears off a mule and
mostly about bills bills bills or about how men, especially
her husband Fred, weren't worth shooting. Of course,
with Fred, it was the truth. Shiftless and no good and a
wife-beater into the bargain. Spent his days down at the
pool hall and his nights crawling after any woman on
two legs who would have him. A cut from the same cloth,
Ella Mae thought, as her very own daddy. Though,
thank the good Lord, her mama had been spared the
knowledge. Or pretended to know nothing; you never
knew with Mama. There was so much she never said, so
much she kept hidden. So much that she took with her
into the grave, poor thing.

Ella Mae was grateful her own marriage had escaped
that awful fate. Edward had his faults, what man didn't,
but he had never done anything vile and depraved, he
wasn't the reprobate her own daddy was. She sat at the
table, wiping away a fresh slide of tears with the backside
of her hand. She looked at her ring finger and thought

again about trying to get the ring off with soap or maybe some Jergens Lotion. It hurt, the ring did, much as she denied it to herself and Edward. She was going to have to go to the clinic, if they'd have her, and get a doctor to saw it off. The flesh was way up over the wedding band, sometimes so bad you could hardly see it, and the skin had a purplish tinge. She'd seen the same thing happen on the farm where her daddy had lashed a piece of barbed wire around a tree. Years later there would be a thin line in the bark but the wire would have disappeared. So she'd have to go soon else her finger would fall off.

Still, she hated the thought of someone taking a saw to her hand. Hated the thought of her wedding band being cut in half. It hurt but she guessed she could stand it. She'd feel naked, she knew, without her ring. It meant all the world to her. "So," she said aloud, "I'll just put up with it, I'll give it another year. If I have to go out somewhere I can wear gloves, I can buy a new pair and that will hide it."

She shook her hair away from her face, weeping, telling herself that a good cry never hurt anyone. Her purse was on the kitchen table where she'd left it, and she dug inside for her compact mirror. She brought out the compact along with a pile of loose tissues and, to her surprise, a Bit-o-Honey candy bar. "Land-sakes," she said to herself, "I must have been carrying around that candy for a coon's age." On it were lint and fluff and grains of dirt, sand it looked like, though she couldn't see how sand had got there. About half of the bar had been eaten. She put it down, and examined her face and hair in the dusty mirror. Well, she thought, smiling at herself, her lips pushed back, I still have nice teeth. I still have pretty hair. Her hair was fluffy and thick and midnight black, with not a lick of gray yet, discounting a few patches at the roots. Edward already had a gray band over his ears and his sideburns were gray when he let them grow. Not that he ever did because Edward had got used to short hair in the Navy and he liked to keep pretty much to what he called a butch cut—a shaved head, the boys called it. He didn't mind the gray, he said it made him look dignified, which it did, of course. And the butch cut, he said, kept him looking young.

The boys didn't like their own hair cut that way, they complained that kids at school called them "skinheads" and worse. She had to tell them there was nothing she could do about it, they'd have to put up with it and not let it get their goats, because nothing put Edward in a bad temper so much as long hair on his own children. Or on anyone else, for that matter. "You can go to the barber," he'd tell them, "or you can move your belongings out into the street." Naturally, he didn't mean the boys were actually to go to a professional barber, they'd jump at that. No, they were to go to their mama and she'd cut their hair the same as she'd always done.

Ella Mae unwrapped the candy bar without thinking, reflecting on the number of times she'd got out the scissors and a towel and a pan of cold water to cut their hair, while they squirmed and yelled and complained so much the neighbors must have thought they were killing each other. She had tried leaving an inch or two on the top and some color on the sides, though it did no good. Edward just sent them back with orders to take more off. She guessed it was one of his funny notions of being a man—though he didn't mind Billy Graham's hair or Pat Boone's and he admitted Rock Hudson's long hair looked all right on him. "Oh, menfolks," her mama would say, "there's no understanding or explaining them, so you'd best not try." He liked *her* hair. She couldn't count the times he'd come up behind her and run his hand through her hair or sniffed it after she'd shampooed, telling her what a beautiful head of hair she had. *Tresses,* he'd say. "I haven't seen tresses that full on a woman since my ship pulled out of Japan. Now *there* was women who knew how to grow hair."

"I guess that wasn't all they knew," she'd say.

He'd leer and stand back on his heels and tell her she'd said a mouthful. A plain Tom Fool, Edward was, able to put her in stitches anytime he had a mind to.

She had been absentmindedly picking the fuzz off the Bit-o-Honey and now she broke off a wedge and plopped it in her mouth. The candy was hard—like a brick, she thought—but that's how Bit-o-Honey was, fresh or not. She could feel on her tongue the dry fuzz she'd missed, and passed up a temptation to spit it out. Her teeth could make no impression in the candy and she pushed the heel of her hand against her jaw to help them out. She chewed and her jaw ached but she kept on chewing, surprised that it would take so long for the juices to spread around. She tried to figure out how long the candy had been in her purse. Not long, because not more than two weeks ago she'd cleaned out her purse and thrown away a bagful of soiled mints and chewing gum, brown apple cores and sesame-seed crackers and even a banana peel. That was the day Edward had paced the kitchen, a hand cocked behind his right ear, listening for squeaks in the flooring and saying something was going to have to be done about it. He'd gone to the refrigerator and stood in front of it, lifting up one leg after the other like a skinny bird, and she'd heard herself the gnawing sound under him—not that she needed to because she had already told him before he put down the new linoleum that the floor was giving in spots and needed bolstering. He'd had his mind set on linoleum-laying and hadn't been listening. But that day he'd come in cross

about something that had happened down at the yard—
Hargroves was laying off men is what it was—and he'd
been picky-picky about everything and finally had settled on the floor to fuss about.

"Yessir," he'd said, "it can't bear the traffic, it needs
fixing." And by *traffic* she knew he meant *her,* and had got
her feelings hurt, even raising her voice to him, arguing
that a floor was made to hold up people and if his
couldn't hold up her then she reckoned she could stay
upstairs in her bedroom and never come out and let him
make his own dinner and see how he liked that. "Go
ahead and say it," she told him. "I know you want to say
it's my fault, that it's because I'm so large is why the
floor is groaning now." He wasn't used to her talking to
him like that, although to his credit he hadn't got angry.
He'd put on a kind of sneaky grin as if to say he'd raised
the fuss in the first place only to get her goat. He had
pulled up a corner of the linoleum and studied the wood
and in the end agreed with her that maybe it was a little
bit rotten. She'd told him she was sorry and he had
laughed, saying she had the feelings of a young colt, she
was just high-strung, no need to get on her high horse
and start talking about locking herself in bedrooms.

"On the other hand," he'd said, leering, circling
around her, "if you want to pay a quick visit to it before
the boys come home, I reckon I'm available." And he
had done a little shuffle of his feet, what he called his Ali
shuffle, at the same time hitching up his pants that were
weighted down with hammers and screwdrivers and
such.

She had to forget her crossness then, for his saying that
had brought everything back to her, his courtly ways,
and made her feel young again. She had even let him get
her halfway up the stairs, the two of them laughing, her
screeching and smacking at his hands because he kept
trying to goose her. But no farther than halfway, since it

was still daylight and since the boys *would* choose that minute to come streaking in. Just, she now supposed, as he had counted on.

She had to give up on the Bit-o-Honey. It refused to chew, and the little headway she could make on it was almost pulling her teeth out. Her jaws hurt. The effort was beginning to give her a headache; she'd get lockjaw if she kept on. As she opened the garbage can, intending to spit it out, some sight outside the sink window, nothing more perhaps than the way a tree limb scooped low to the ground or the way the black utility lines sagged low on their poles, reminded her of those days of childhood poverty when the purchase of a candy bar might be her major transaction in any one full year, with one Christmas starting that year and the next one ending it and there being nothing in between but emptiness, emptiness and yearning—nor anything to mark Christmas that wasn't homemade or handed down. Miserable times. Unforgivable times. Preacher Eelbone had gone out of his way trying to explain it, but it still beat her why God wanted so many poor people in the world or why He seemed to go out of His way to keep them poor. God might strike her with a thunderbolt, He might send one down this very minute to slice her open and pay her back for thinking that way, but He'd just have to do it if that was His will, nothing was going to change her mind. Then she found herself laughing. Remembering that they had had to go out in the freezing cold of a winter night to visit the toilet, and use slick Sears catalog paper or maybe even a corncob if the Wish Book had run out. "Well, we'd best order something," she could remember her mama saying, "else they won't send us a free catalog next year. *Then* what will we use?"

She stood, chuckling, wondering what her boys would say if she took away all their fine winter coats and their Star Wars creatures and fitted them up in longjohns and made them scratch their games in the dirt the way she and Edward had to do. They wouldn't put up with it, they'd howl and raise a stink and probably murder their parents and, likely as not, the Supreme Court would side with them. That's what Edward would say. He'd say they were spoiled rotten, they had no more backbone than a snake, that with them it was all *Gimme Gimme Gimme.*

Still, they were sweet boys and you couldn't fault them none that times had changed.

She came out of her trance to find Eula Joyner's hawk face tacked up and hung over her sink window. Then Eula's fingers came up and rattled on the glass, with a "Yoo-hoo!" thrown in.

Ella Mae went over and raised the window to let Eula stick her head in. Eula would never visit inside a person's house, being afraid she'd be thought of as lazy and no-account, with nothing to do at home. She had a scarf tied around her head, decorated with green flamingos, and Ella Mae could tell by her height that she had on Fred's cowboy boots.

"I got me six thousand Green Stamps," Eula said. "I been counting them all morning but I run out of books. You don't have any, do you?"

Ella Mae pulled up a stool. There was no telling whether her neighbor would stay a minute or three hours. She said no, she didn't have any spare books, and asked Eula what she planned on getting with her stamps.

"I don't know. Last time I got this scarf which cost only one book. You ought to get yourself one. Of course, if I know Edward he'd raise a stink if he knew you were out getting yourself a nice kerchief when he could be using those same stamps for a wrench or a set of pliers. That's men for you."

"I never said I wanted a scarf, Eula."

"I saw him up at the window. I saw that thing he put up. What's it for?"

Ella Mae watched resentfully as smoke poured from Eula's nostrils. She was always having to defend Edward before this woman. It looked to her like a woman who had a man like Fred to contend with would naturally keep her mouth shut about another woman's husband. But not Eula.

"I told Fred it was tacky, first thing you know it will bring down our property value, that's what I told Fred. Don't it make it kind of dark in your bedroom? Is he going to put one over the boys' window too? That wouldn't keep it from looking tacky, but at least it wouldn't make the house so lopsided-looking. Frankly, I think he's lost his marbles this time."

Ella Mae was in no mood to listen to Eula's opinions. She felt at the mercy of her nerves and knew she'd feel better with something to eat in her hands—though not with Eula Joyner looking on. Eula was skinny as a handrail and her little hawk eyes missed nothing. She liked to brag that she didn't weigh a hundred pounds and even that looked heavy on her. "My system's delicate," she'd say. "Can't hold anything down, and never could."

"I see you run into your hedge," she was now saying. "I was looking out the window when you came zigzagging by, and I said to myself at the time, 'Well, Ella

Mae's going to wreck that truck before she gets out of it,'
and be darned if you didn't go almost smack through the
hedge. I guess Edward pretty near killed you."

Ella Mae said no, a person of Edward's mild disposi-
tion wasn't liable to be bothered, and anyway she hadn't
damaged the hedge.

"I'd take down that hedge if I were you. Lot of clutter,
seems to me. As you know, I like a bare yard, I like a yard
that lets you see things."

Ella Mae nodded. A few years back, Eula and Fred
had got four old tractor tires from the city dump. They
had rolled them out over the rocks and red dirt in front
of their trailer, and where the tires fell they'd put in
chicken manure and a little earth and stuck in a few
flowers. The flowers had lasted a week or two, then died,
but the tractor tires were still there. Sometimes they'd
come out and sit on them. Except for the tires and one
stunted umbrella tree, their yard was indeed bare.

"Of course each to his own, I say. If folks were all alike,
I'd just as soon chop off my head—that's what I tell
Fred." The cigarette smoke flared through her nostrils.
She reached a bony arm through Ella Mae's window and
dropped her smoking butt into the sink. "How come
you're not eating?"

Ella Mae murmured that she had no appetite. Eula let
out a disbelieving squawk. "Are you *sick?*"

"Can't a person just not be hungry?" Ella Mae asked,
piqued.

"I don't know about that. But I never saw you without
something in your hand."

Ella Mae was too hurt by this to speak. There really
was something about this woman that she didn't like,
and as much as she tried to conquer her revulsion, she
saw little chance of making any headway today. She had
half a mind to tell her to go on home.

"Of course with our bills, it's a good thing I eat like a bird. Fred won't work, I guess you know that. He's over there now snoring away in bed. That's men for you."

"Well, we've all got bills, Eula."

"He put in three days down at the yard last month, and he drank all that up. I still don't know how he got by me. I was down at the gate waiting for him to come out with his paycheck but he got by me and the next time I saw him he was drunk. I think he must of gone over the fence in the back."

"Maybe he ought to go to that drying-out place again."

"He won't go," said Eula, exasperated. "He used to like it because there was always someone to sneak a bottle in, but they've clamped down now so he won't go. He'd rather stay around here and live off me and drive me into an early grave. If I didn't make him he wouldn't even bathe."

"I know you're good to him, Eula."

"His own mama threw him out twenty years ago. He was worthless and no-account then and he still is. I remind him of that every day just to see what he'll do. Last night he come at me with a stick of lit firewood but I took it away from him easy as a baby. Did you hear the dogfight last night?"

Ella Mae said no, she hadn't.

"They were really going at it, right outside my window it sounded like. It's things like that can bring down property values faster than a person can think. I'm surprised you didn't hear it."

Ella Mae again said no, she hadn't, and asked whose dogs they were.

"Not ours, if that's what you're thinking. If our dogs behaved that way I'd shoot them."

Fred kept eight dogs he sometimes used for hunting in

a small pen at the rear of the trailer. They occasionally
barked the entire night through because Eula and Fred
would forget to feed them.

"How's your finger?"

Ella Mae had got out potatoes, she'd washed them,
and now was peeling them with a paring knife. "It's all
right," she said.

"Lord, you eat a lot of potatoes."

"There are four of us, Eula. You don't know what it
takes to fill a growing boy's stomach."

"Is Ike and Theodore home yet?" asked Eula. "School
must have let out long ago. I hope you've got your eye on
them. There's a gang, you know, meets after school on
the playground and they go out and steal hubcaps and
car batteries. I'd lock the truck if I were you, at night I
mean. I read about it in the paper." She lit another cigarette, stuck it between her lips, then took off her scarf and
retied it around her head. Eula's hair was like wire, what
little she had. It grew in patches—Ella Mae thought this
was because she never let it get any sunshine. "Fred says
they caught the ringleader but he was from a well-to-do
family so it was hushed up. I don't reckon you and Edward would be so lucky." Smoke drifted into her eyes;
she was squinting down at Ella Mae's large spread of potato peels as if she didn't think much of the job her
neighbor was doing.

"My boys don't steal, Eula."

"That much potatoes would keep Fred and me fed for
a month," Eula said. She thumped out her ashes into the
sink and backed up a few paces into the yard, her way of
telling Ella Mae that she'd wasted all the time she could.
"That Edward!" she said. "He's got boards spread out
all over your front yard. I call that plain tacky."

"I'll tell him about it, Eula. I wouldn't want you to
blame us if your property value comes down."

"I wish you would. Why is it men can't pick up after

themselves is a riddle to me. Fred has got his boxers and his sweat shirt at the foot of the bed where he kicked them a week ago. That's a man for you." She started off, but turned back. "How are your feet?" she asked. "I saw the way you were walking in them shoes when you came back from the store." She kicked one foot high, as if to tell Ella Mae she ought to come to her senses and get herself a good pair of cowboy boots.

"I get by," Ella Mae said. "I reckon as long as I'm meant to walk I'll walk."

"Fred uses Odor-Eaters in his shoes—not that they help in that line—says it makes his shoes more comfortable. Edward told him that you'd gone off your diet, that your heart was getting squeezed. Is that right? Anyway, that's why I asked. I hear tell there's something inside certain people that makes them eat, the same way people who like to drink have to have their alcohol. I saw that in the paper, must have been a week ago. Real good story."

"I missed that."

"They say that's why a fat person stays fat. Some doctor wrote it."

"I'm not fat, Eula. I'm a naturally large woman."

"I wasn't hinting anything. Did Edward get that trouble with the floor figured out?"

"It's good as new now, Eula. You can see how good the linoleum looks."

"We don't have any linoleum in our place. Our trailer was one of the first made, it's got real hardwood floors. It's birdseye maple, one of the hardest woods known to man. I ought to know, I have to scrub it often enough. Did Edward get what he wanted out of that TV?"

"I guess so, Eula."

"I saw him drive off in the truck. Going back to the yard, I guess. Is he getting laid off too?"

"They wouldn't lay off Edward, Eula. He practically runs that place."

"I hope not. Bills is one thing, but having your man underfoot all day is ten times worse. I'd be a happy woman if I—"

Ella Mae didn't hear the rest. Eula was already striding across the yard, her body pitched forward from the waist up, her heels leaving holes like hoofprints in the dirt.

She pulled the window back down. She'd weathered Eula's visit. She was safe until tomorrow.

She went to the hall closet, the one under the stairs, poking around in the dark, lifting out brooms and mops and various pails and the old butter churn that had belonged to her mama. She stood these in the hall and, on her knees, reached deep into the closet, reached under an empty box that had been turned upside-down, and slid out her scales. The exertion tired her, blood rushed to her face, and she remained a moment on her knees, folded over like someone in prayer. When her breathing was normal she hoisted herself up by the doorway, and with one foot slid the scales the rest of the way into the hall. She went back into the kitchen to lock the door, then to the front to do the same.

She placed one foot lightly on the scales, groaning as the black numerals whirled past the arrow. Before the dial completed its spin she lifted that leg off, stepped to the side, saw the numbers whirling, and placed her other foot down. The numbers braked, began spinning back. She removed that foot too; the dial tried to adjust, whirling like crazy again. This was weight, this was all weight was, this is what one could do with weight. Quickly she stepped on with both feet. The machine sank down under her, creaking loudly, protesting, as much as admitting that it was beaten. Head uplifted, eyes shut tight, she spread her hands against the wall for support. She could hear the dial jiggling, the squeak of springs, the metal square on which she stood folding with her as she gave more weight to one leg or the other. It came to her that she was holding her breath out. So she sucked in a big mouthful of air, immediately regretting it, for she could sense the numerals rolling by—another pound, another pound. She knew this machine well; it could purr or hiss and spit like a cat. She knew there was no trusting it, that the number it finally put there had nothing to do with her, told nothing about who she was. She carried it, the weight, but it was not her. She kept her eyes squeezed closed. She could forget everything, she could be slender as a thread, a soft wind could lift her up and blow her along and put her down again with nothing broken, with no leaf damaged, no skin bruised. The runoff from even the smallest rain could carry her along. Her arms were tired. She looked at the wall. Her fingers were tense, clinging to that flat surface, trying to lift herself up, to pack her weight into the wall and the ceiling and, ultimately, into the sky, where it would be as nothing. Weight becoming nothing, becoming air, air meeting air, air existing as nothing more than air which one could breathe to heart's content and be satisfied, even rewarded. The black and white face of the dial was silent, the scales steady, inviting her to look down, the silence reminding her that this was only a machine, man-made and therefore useless, that its black numerals were meaningless and at the same time innocent, they meant her no harm.

But she wouldn't look just yet. She feared what might be there: the dial spun full circle, spun back to that dead weight, that 0 it showed at the start. All the way past all the numbers, limitless, all of it hers. She hesitated, in agony, feeling her weight increasing. That was the trouble with scales, the weight the arrow pointed to was never your real weight, you knew you weighed less or more. Times like this, putting off that moment when she would have to look down, her legs began to feel like trees.

No, worse than that—like massive sawed-off tree trunks that you could make tables from to seat twelve. Great pillars of reinforced concrete, stanchions into which poured not just her own rightful weight but the weight of the room and its furniture as well. They took everything and tried to make her believe the weight shown at the arrow was hers only. This was not fair. God should not make a fool of her this way.

She could stand the torture no more and did at last look down, though only momentarily, a fleeting glance at the dial as she stepped back clumsily off the scales, at the same moment flinging her hands over her eyes for good measure, saying to herself *I refuse to, I'll not be made a fool of, I was crazy to get on this machine in the first place, I'll know better next time.* She pitched the pails, the mops and brooms back inside the closet. Slammed the door.

In the kitchen she pulled out a chair and sat gratefully down, one hand pressing against her chest because she imagined she could feel the squeeze that Edward went on about. She was perspiring, and wiped her brow with the hem of her dress. The material came away unclean, which perplexed and shamed her because, Lord knows, she was not a person who forgot to wash herself. On her chest, her hand lifted and fell, lifted and fell. She watched it—in time, tickled, finding proof here that her heart was strong: it could push so much flesh, it could heave her swollen breasts and her hand and her other hand too if she was of a mind to put it there.

She sat up straight, wiping the flat of her hand across the table's smooth top. She had wanted a Formica table with chrome and plastic on the chairs, but Edward's view had prevailed. He could make a table, he said, making a table was the easiest thing in the world, anyone with a lick of sense could bolt four legs to a frame and find good wood—pine or cedar or maybe even birdseye maple if the Joyners would let him tear up their floor—

to dress up the top. "But I don't want a plain old wooden table," she had said, "I want yellow Formica with aluminum edging. I don't want to be country anymore. I don't want people in this town poking ridicule at me."

"You'll like my table," he had replied, "just because it's wood doesn't mean it can't be nice. We don't have to carve our initials in it and if you want it shiny, we can make it shiny. I can coat it with so much lacquer you can see yourself smile."

So here it was twenty years later, nicked here and there by the boys, but she could still see herself. She could even see herself smile, remembering how this table came to be. Remembering how she came to be here with a right to sit at it, with a good man for a husband and with most of their bills paid, and two children thrown in to bless it all. So why did she feel so lonely, so abused and violated and practically condemned? Why did she sometimes feel hatred and meanness rushing in on her, foaming inside her like a Viola Dodson shampoo? Why did it sweep in, that desire to race across the street fast as she could and hurl herself against the front of Eula Joyner's trailer and send it crashing flat to the ground? Eula was a busybody, she looked like trash with her head tied up and her little raw hawk eyes, but what true harm had she ever done anyone? *When have I ever seen you without food in your hand? I've heard fat people are like drunkards, they can't help eating. Read it in the news.* No one in her right mind would want to flatten someone's house for nothing more damaging than these little old remarks. She'd have to make it up to Eula somehow. Eula had her troubles too, worse troubles. Why blame her for what appears in the news? Burl Ives suffers too. He goes to Duke University to eat rice. I can read newspapers too. I know what is going on in the world. I know I'm not alone. I've got Bette Wiffle in Antigonish, Nova Scotia. That makes two of us having the time of our lives. I'm living it up here in my kitchen waiting for my boys to get home, waiting to learn some reason why my husband has put boards over my bedroom window. Now when I'm up there I'll have only myself to see, nothing else can come in. Maybe that's why he's done it. Maybe he means it as a punishment to me. Maybe God has appeared to him in a dream and said *Edward, Edward, board up your wife's window. She's seen enough of God's handiwork. Do it, Edward, or I'll pluck out your eyes!* Maybe. Why not? Stranger things happen. And Edward would see no harm in it, a view meant nothing to him. To him all it meant was seeing things. If he could see it there was a chance he could get to it, and if he could get that close there was always the chance he'd find something he could use.

He found me, I've been *it* all my life. Taking me apart, looking to find the parts that are of use to him. *All day for one rusty bolt or one squeezed heart, Ella Mae, but worth the effort, I guess.*

Edward, Edward, Edward, she thought, staring at her ring finger mounted against the shiny tabletop like a trophy over glass, why aren't you here now taking care of me? Convincing me, like you used to, that things may be bad, but still better than worse, and more than people who come from where we come from ever thought or dreamed they'd have.

She got the butter churn from the hall, placing it by her chair in the kitchen. She spread her legs, pushed down her dress, and dragged the churn up between her knees. She lifted the lid out over the handle and peered inside. Cobwebs, a few dead flies, one or two shriveled spiders. The churn was handmade, black walnut, she thought, and her mama must have bought it off someone or inherited it herself because her daddy would never have known how or been willing to make one. She lifted the churn up to her nose, closed her eyes, and let herself breathe it in. Musky, but you could still smell the butter. The wood had a soft buttery feel which came off on her finger.

Her poor mama. She had sat with this thing between her legs and churned and churned and she had enjoyed it, the churning, because it took her mind off things, it let her mind roam. It was good exercise for her arms, and for her stomach too once the butter thickened.

Hard work had kept her mama thin.

Of course, it had killed her too.

The potatoes, not yet cut up for home fries, had turned brown. "I best get at it," she said in Edward's voice, reaching for the knife. "I best see what's left in these I can use."

A few minutes later the boys caterwauled in, slamming the door and colliding with each other as they scrambled down the hall, colliding again as they reached the doorway at the same instant. There they hung, screeching like broken parts, each trying to squeeze the other out.

"Hush," she told them. "How many times I told you to behave?"

They paid her no mind, of course. They in no way noticed her at all. They scooted in a slide over the linoleum, punching and calling each other names, now yelling that they were hungry, what was there to eat? They flung open the refrigerator door with such violence the entire room shook; one stood fanning the cold air over his face while the other crawled between his legs, emerging with a head of cabbage, which he attempted to stuff down his brother's pants. Before she could reach them they rolled away. The older boy dove for the bread box, pulled out a new loaf she had bought that day, and gave it a judo chop down the middle. The ends of the bag burst open and from both directions the sliced bread fanned to the floor. He picked up a handful of what remained and tried to cram a fistful into his jaws while the other shoved and pulled, wanting that fistful for himself. They kicked at the bread on the floor, shrieking, never looking at her but escaping by instinct alone as she bore down on them. Then, as quickly as they had come, they now shot away, colliding in the hall, slamming the door once, twice, their cries now muted, finally emptying out altogether as they streaked off to watch some friend's TV or to steal the hubcaps off Eula Joyner's dusty Chevrolet that was up on blocks and had been for five years.

Boys. They would be boys. With girls a parent at least had a faint chance; with boys it was best to throw your hands up at the start, to say All right, you're boys, I give up! The house is yours, my life is yours, wreck both any way you want to.

She shook her head at the ruin they had made this time, amazed as she always was by such energy, by the juices flowing in them that weren't Hopkins juices or her juices or anybody else's juices that she could name. Alonso Draper, crazy as a bedbug and locked up at Dorothea Dix Asylum before he was fourteen years old or out of first grade, maybe his.

Boys, yes. But by what right could she blame them for being what they had to be, for wanting to have their fun? She couldn't blame them any more than she could blame Bette Wiffle up there in Antigonish, Nova Scotia, or blame Eula Joyner for taking to cowboy boots. That had been her own daddy's mistake, it was one Edward often shared. *Go and stand in that corner for three days. Put your hand in this bucket of ice water, and if I see you just once flinch, you'll get my fist against your face. Down on your knees, girl, and keep licking my boots until you learn to stop knocking over your glass.* Well, Edward wasn't that bad, though her daddy had been. Mama standing by, glaring, maybe even raising a broom, saying *Don't you harm a hair of that girl's head.*

She got supper going. Her finger was acting up. Every five minutes or so she stopped to immerse it in a pan of warm water. She took one aspirin and broke it in half and took that. She had heard about people taking pills, maybe Eula had told her (*read it in the paper, read it in the paper*), and didn't want herself becoming dependent on them. She had enough pills already, her diet pills, which did no good, and her nerve pills, which made her worse. But something would have to be done about the finger. She knew she wouldn't be able to sleep tonight. She'd be up and down, up and down, making Edward cross, and wasting electricity. She could come downstairs and sleep on the sofa, of course. But it would break her heart to do that. She never had. The thought of Edward up there alone in bed, his knees bent to tuck up under hers—the idea tickled her it was so out of the question.

So sad, too. A husband and wife who didn't sleep in the same bed. Well, anything could happen next. And usually did. No, she'd just have to put up with the hurt finger and do her best to lie still. Edward needed his sleep, it took rest to do the heavy work he did at the yard. Frail, you wouldn't think he could walk to the corner, but she had seen him lift a hundred-pound sack of seed or cement with the same ease tobacco fiends could lift their cigarettes. Last winter, showing off how he could drive in the snow, he'd wrapped the truck's rear end into a ditch not one foot away from a telephone pole. While other folks were calling for tow trucks to remove their stranded cars, Edward had got down on his knees under the bumper with a board on his shoulder to keep the metal from cutting him, and he'd just lifted that truck up on his back and planted it down again on level ground.

Of course, it had been a long time since he had lifted her. It had been a long time, she reckoned, since he'd been able to get his arms to meet around her.

She went out into the front yard to bring in the boys' jackets and their lunch boxes. She went through the pockets looking for homework assignments or test papers, but she found nothing other than the usual assortment of nuts and bolts, for in that line they were as bad as Edward. They hadn't eaten their fruit, she noticed. Ike had stuck a stick through his orange, and little Theodore had written all over his, though she couldn't make out what it said. His writing was hardly legible in the first place and why he thought he could write on an orange so anybody could read it was beyond her. She'd have to get Edward to talk to them again about the scurvy, about how could they expect to be good athletes if they didn't eat their fruit. Well, no, better hold off on that, no need making Edward mad, reminding him of the money that was wasted around here.

She checked the rosebush close up, wishing Edward would be more careful with her yard. It seemed to be all right. She guessed it would survive. The ladder was still leaning against the house, leading right up to her bedroom window. She wondered if she could manage it. If she would dare. Eula Joyner would be looking, maybe some of the other neighbors as well; she knew they'd be laughing at her, their faces pressed to fence or window, just waiting for the minute she fell so they could come running over to tell her what a sight she was making of herself. She put one foot on a lower rung and shook the ladder; it seemed firm enough. It seemed strong enough. It wasn't likely a good two-by-four couldn't hold up even her. She'd try it. Go up three or four rungs just to see if that nearer view wouldn't tell her more about what Edward was doing. She couldn't see any hinges and without hinges it wasn't likely he meant for the boards to swing open. It looked to her, from down here, that he'd nailed the boards square into the house. As if he meant them to be permanent. But that was just plain crazy.

On the third step up she rested. She felt a little giddy. She never had been much of a climber. From time to time she looked back over her shoulder, but could see no one watching. If they were, she decided, they were hidden.

She wished the boys were here so she could send one of them up.

She went slowly up two more. Her ring finger was hurting because she had had to use it to hold on, and her bare foot had picked up a splinter. She hugged the ladder. It seemed to her that she was stuck there, not willing to look up and having learned already—the taste of bile had rushed up her throat—that it was a mistake to look down. The edges cut into her skin. One of her legs began a nervous quiver; she felt faint, and for a second was afraid she'd fall.

She became aware that someone was watching her. She managed, by degrees, to turn her head. It was the paper boy, standing on the edge of her grass, holding his hands on his hips, just watching.

"Scat!" she said.

He shrugged, threw the tubed newspaper up on the
front steps, and ambled on, whistling.

Ella Mae in time found the strength to come back
down. It was anger that did it. "Edward with his plans,"
she muttered aloud. "Edward with his secrets! If I had
him here now I'd choke him."

Inside again, she checked
the stove, then set the table. She got out the good china
and put that down, although she couldn't explain to
herself exactly why. She got out the silver—*EG* was en-
graved on it—that Edward had bought for their tenth
wedding anniversary out of a magazine and that had not
been used more than five times since. Well, she knew
why. She was using it tonight because the boys and Edward both had made her mad. She was saving this silver
for the boys when they got married, but if they were
going to throw bread all over her kitchen and then light
out without so much as a simple how-do-you-do, then
they didn't deserve it.

She put the folded newspaper by Edward's plate—it
wouldn't surprise her none if tomorrow the headline
read ELLA MAE HOPKINS TRIED TO CLIMB A LADDER BUT
COULDN'T—and got out linen napkins, still in their box
with the hard plastic top, and placed these around the
table.

She wished she had candles to light, but Edward
wouldn't sit still for that.

She squared the chairs off just right, then stood back
to appraise the job she'd done.

She wished her mama was here to see it.

Poor Mama, the only silver she had ever owned was the locket she wore around her neck till the day she died—when her daddy had cut it off her neck with his pocket knife and jammed it in his pocket, saying as how he reckoned the little woman would have no more need for that.

She wondered whose neck that locket was around now.

She wondered if her mama at some point hadn't opened her eyes to the darkness and said that she wanted it back.

Ella Mae turned her back on the table to have herself a good cry. "Here I am crying," she said aloud, "like a war widow, like I have so many reasons I don't even know the reasons I have. Like some poor miserable woman who never sees sunshine. I would trade all my riches and take on a dozen worries more just to have Mama's locket here in my hand. The boys wouldn't, but Edward would, because Mama, I know how much you would have liked him had you lived to see him. Had you stayed on, Mama, to set your mind at ease, knowing I was in good hands."

That was one of the griefs of her life, that Mama had been denied the pleasure of getting to know Edward.

She got out the Ungentine, which for convenience' sake, she kept in the silverware drawer, and spread the salve over her finger. The inflamed skin grown up around her ring seemed to pulse and it brought new tears to her eyes to touch it. It gave off heat like a naked light bulb and she thought it so ugly she could hardly bear to look at it. She closed her eyes, thinking about shooting

up a quick prayer to God, but decided it would be con-
temptible of her to approach God over something she
alone was responsible for. She had put it off and put it
off and now she'd just have to put up with it.

She washed her face in the sink and told herself she
felt better. She swept her potato peels and other scraps
into the garbage. She hated doing that; such a waste, she
thought. She stayed a moment that way, staring down
into the garbage, remembering how in her day all such
cooking and table scraps went into the slop pail and she
had to tote it down to the pens every evening and empty
it into the trough. She hated having to haul it down that
dark path every night, of course, because some of it was
bound to splash on your legs. It looked and smelled terrible, and it had beat her how a living thing could eat it.
But she'd enjoyed the sounds the hogs made, their crazy
enthusiasm for everything from watermelon rind to coffee grounds. They'd just jump right into the trough, their
delicate round little feet sliding every which way, oink-
oinking, slurping, trying to root each other out, their
small bright eyes shining. They were stupid, those hogs
and pigs, and ugly as sin, but they had certainly enjoyed
their swill and you couldn't blame them for that.

The floor creaked. She turned, and there stood Ike
studying her with hooded eyes.

"What's that out yonder?" he asked, jabbing a balled-
up filthy hand over his shoulder.

"Out where, honey?"

"Out yonder," the boy repeated, his voice put out with
her.

"Out yonder where?"

"Out yonder!" he suddenly screamed. *"Out yonder on the
house! Them boards on the window!"*

She wanted to shake him. To get her hands on him
and shake him.

"It looks stupid," the boy said. "I never saw anything looked so stupid. I climbed up on the ladder and looked at it and it looks stupid. It's stupid, that's all." He paused, his eyes glazed, waiting to see whether she would agree with him. "Eula says so too. Eula says it's plain stupid."

He spun on his heels and walked out, kicking at the doorway as he went through.

She would have to tell Edward. That's all there was to it, she would have to tell Edward and hope he wouldn't take a strap to him. Ike and Theodore were having growing pains, that was all, they'd soon grow out of this nothing-can-please-us stage. They were naturally sweet boys, just feeling themselves now. All boys were the same.

Still, she wished they'd sometimes smile when they spoke to her. She wished they'd learn to show a little human warmth. That they'd cuddle up sometimes to her like they'd done no more than a year or two ago. Nowadays when she got close enough to them to try and give them a kiss, they'd roll their faces away and say something like "Ugh, I'd puke." Edward would laugh, he'd guffaw and slap his knees, hearing them say that. *They only joking, Ella Mae. No need to get your haunches up.* And Eula Joyner was as bad. No, you never could get any neighborly comfort out of complaining to her. She'd say, *It's your own fault, fool! You been spoiling their britches rotten. If I had them two, I'd tie them to a hot stove till I burned some of their sassiness off.*

There was one to talk. Sassy as a jaybird herself, and so wrapped up in her own bounty she went to sleep every night kissing her dollar bills. *She ain't much,* Fred would say, *but at least she's thrifty!* If a cripple fell in a ditch, she'd walk across the road and kick him rather than help him out. She'd been too selfish ever to have children herself.

*Lord, I'd as soon have me a skunk-hog pulling at my teats. A
child is hardly human until he comes to his puberty that's what I
read one time in a book.* If Eula Joyner had ever seen a book,
it would be one that had Green Stamps in it.

Her mama used to tell her that children were God's
way of rewarding and punishing a woman. That the
woman who didn't weigh punishment against reward
every day of her life might as well head straight for the
lunatic asylum. "Take you, for instance," she'd say.
"You're nothing but trouble. Yet I wouldn't trade you
for anything in the world. Not for gold mine or sultan's
palace, not for the whole of the Sears Wish Book. I
wouldn't even trade your daddy and for that maybe *I*
ought to be in the asylum—but without him you'd have
been someone else. You'd be some slanty-eyed child I
wouldn't know from Adam. Mind you, I'd *improve* on
him a bit. If I had my way, I'd put that thing growing
between his legs in a vise and I'd squeeze it tight as I
could. I'd put those fists of his in brine and let them cook
until they couldn't hurt me no more. I'd drain the alcohol out of him and fix it so if he touched another drop
he'd go screaming into hell. And if this was heaven and
not earth, I wouldn't stop there. I'd fix it so I'd have
more time to myself, so I wouldn't have to go go go from
sunrise to sunset. But, no, there ain't a thing I'd change
in you. I'd take some of that weight off, that's all. I'd
want you to have *now* the beauty I know you're going to
have *some* day."

Poor Mama. One good thing about Mama being dead
was that she didn't have to know her little girl's beauty
had never come. What little there was had all been in her
own and in her mama's sweet head.

The phone rang, jangling these thoughts from her mind. She had to run and hope she'd make it. The phone was all the way down the hall and through the living room and into the den, where you had to look for it because Edward was always moving it or piling tools and his loose parts over it. Most times she'd be upstairs making beds or in the bath or out in the back yard, and she'd be so out of breath by the time she reached it that she'd have to pant like a dog and let everybody think they'd dialed the loony bin. More times than not, she just wouldn't make it, which was just as well since it was usually somebody selling toothbrushes or free trips to Hawaii or telling her about the dry-cleaning special they had on this month.

This time it was Edward's boss, Mr. Hargroves. She got that much by straining. Mr. Hargroves had a throat condition—some said it was a yardstick stuck up his you-know-what—and couldn't speak above a whisper.

He was wanting Edward. "But he's at the yard, Mr. Hargroves. If you poke your head out the window you'll probably see him."

"I've looked," said the whisper. "He's not here."

"Why, he *ought* to be!"

"I know he ought, since he's drawing wages regular as rain, but the fact is we haven't seen him since lunch. He's been acting queer lately, you want to know the truth."

"That sure doesn't sound like my Edward!"

"Anything bothering him, you know of? Homewise, I mean."

"He's been like cotton candy, Mr. Hargroves. Just sweet as a kitten."

Mr. Hargroves stopped talking to her to talk to somebody else about a shipment of green studs, whatever they
were, that had been held up somewhere. Whoever he was
talking to apparently couldn't hear him any better than
she could, since they kept saying *"What—what?"*

Then he was talking to her again.

"He comes in, you tell him to see me first thing in the
morning."

"I will, Mr. Hargroves."

"I been trying to catch him for three days. Every time
I go out in the yard to have a word with him, he seems to
run away. You sure he's got nothing preying on his
mind?"

"He's cheery as a magpie, Mr. Hargroves."

"Of course, we're laying off bunches of men. Could be
it's that. Could be he thinks he's next in line."

"I never heard of such a thing. You wouldn't be fool
enough to lay off Edward."

"Not up to us, Mrs. Hopkins. We do what the head
office over in Eustacia tells us to do. Bleak times though,
that's cold fact. How's your finger?"

She wasn't sure she'd heard him.

"How's that again, Mr. Hargroves?"

"I said how's your finger. Somebody was telling me,
maybe Fred Joyner, you might have to have it ampu-
tated."

She said no, no, Fred or whoever had it all wrong, her
finger was fine, it was pussed for a while but now it was
fine.

"All right. Tell the little firecracker to see me."

Ella Mae heard him hang up. Firecracker, she'd never
heard Edward called that before, and mused on it. She
kept the phone to her ear, waiting. They were on a party
line and for five years she had been wondering who was
on it with them. A second or two passed before she heard

the soft click. True enough, the secret party had been listening again. By tomorrow, she expected, the whole town would be saying Edward had played hooky from his job and was about to be fired.

In the kitchen again, she retrieved the newspaper by Edward's plate. YARD LAYOFF LOOMS, read the headline. Under it was a picture of Mr. Hargroves, with a cigar in his hand so big it couldn't help but hurt his throat. "Bleak times," Mr. Hargroves had told the *Clarion.* "If business doesn't pick up we're going to have to let men go right and left. This place will be like a ghost town when and if the yard has to close down."

The article said nine men had already been let go.

That Edward, she thought. *The roof could cave in but would he tell me?*

She knew what the trouble was, of course. That Mr. Hargroves was no good at his job, he didn't know beans about how the yard worked, and they were losing business every day he stayed on. If they put Edward at his desk, things would turn around in no time flat. It wasn't just her saying so. She didn't know anyone, except maybe Eula Joyner, who didn't agree with that.

Edward had only two places in the world, work and home, and she wondered where he could be. That bit about his acting peculiar worried her some, though it was uncalled for. Except for closing off her bedroom window and leaving wood upstairs in her hall, he'd been peaches and cream, sweeter even than usual.

According to her stove clock, it was nearly time for the five o'clock report. She got her hamburger going and checked the cabbage—another half-hour and they'd be about ready—and pushed aside pots and pans to get at the little Philips. She had to switch it on with a hairpin because Edward had not yet quite finished with it. It was a one-station radio only and Edward had worked on it for six months and blown every fuse in the house three times before he got that much. Working in terms of man-hours spent on it at minimum wage, she reckoned this little toy radio had cost near on two hundred dollars. Of course Edward wouldn't see it that way; he'd say they got it for nothing.

Yet there was no need being picky. If she had to be stranded on a desert island with Robinson Crusoe or Edward, she'd pick Edward every time.

Nothing could beat okra and corn and tomatoes for a good succotash, so she dumped those together in a pot on simmer, stirred the hamburger, and chopped up her onions. She dropped a strip of bacon in the succotash for flavor. She ate one strip herself, raw, without meaning to, though she did have a taste for raw bacon. She got her biscuit dough mixed, her mama's recipe or just a country one, she supposed, and turned on the oven, having decided to make a casserole out of the hamburger. She still had plenty of time. Edward liked his dinner on the table precisely at five-forty-five, winter or summer, and she could count on her fingers the times she'd missed. Eula Joyner thought that was awful late, but Eula—well, she'd just have to excuse Eula. It plumb tired Eula out every evening having to get out a can of cold baked beans and open it and scoop them onto her and Fred's plates, with a slice of white bread to top it off and a glass of sourmash whiskey to wash it down.

The Philips was at last beginning to hum. If it was a heater, she'd told Edward, we'd all freeze to death. He had told her, if God gave you a golden apple, you'd ask Him why it wasn't silver.

Just cut-ups, the two of them.

When she thought of her life with Edward, she sometimes wondered if God didn't have to be a touch jealous of their good fortune and happy times. That was why she figured she'd been having that down-in-the-mouth feeling lately, that fear that she was walking along the precipice of doom and might any minute be shoved over—because she and Edward had filled up their quota of happiness. God was going to put a bag over their heads. He was going to tie the drawstring and put out the lights and that would be all she wrote for the Hopkinses.

"Now for the wrap-up," came the radio announcer's voice, startling her. *"The dollar plunged today. In local news, a yard layoff looms, with ten men already sent home. The Blue Jays were licked on their home grounds last night, and tomorrow the weatherman promises blue skies overhead."*

"I best get out my bathing suit," Ella Mae told him.

"Now for a musical interlude," the man said.

"I'm all ears," she said.

She wondered what it was like being a radio announcer, talking to a thousand people a day, going into their homes while they were undressed or cooking or having a spat with their husbands.

Instead of a musical interlude, some other voice came on and talked about Norfleet's Exxon and U-Haul-It, urging people to bring their cars on down to Five Points for the spring checkup where owners Fleetwood and Norman Shearin promised friendliness and hometown hospitality and service-while-you-wait, all at bottom dollar.

Edward had gone to school with Fleetwood Shearin and wouldn't have let him work on his truck for all the do-re-mi in China. Uppity, Edward said, and he'd let his own daddy rot in an old folks' home without raising a finger.

She put in her casserole and cut out her biscuits with a glass, leaving them out to rise—unnecessary, though she preferred it. Then she washed up a bit, for it was her habit to have the kitchen looking spic-and-span for Edward when he came home.

"Now for an editorial expression," the radio man said, *"with your favorite and mine, Jack Coombs."*

"About time," Ella Mae told him.

She didn't know Jack Coombs, nor did Edward, but one day about two years ago he had shown up on the air with this editorial expression and since then hardly a day had gone by when she hadn't tuned him in. He had a real good voice, so deep it went inside her, and one day before she died she hoped she'd be able to shake his hand. He was against unprecedented government spending, just as she and Edward were, and he was concerned about law and order in the streets and maintaining a tight-knit family unit, and he made no bones about his belief that the courts ought to have no say on the practice of religion in our schools. He thought morals were far too lax, just as she and Edward did. He had no use for strong central government except in wartime, the plight of our mail service was an unmentionable crime, and while he wasn't opposed to paying his share of high taxes he wanted assurance his money was well spent and that his vote counted and he was not misrepresented by a bunch of do-gooders and bleeding-heart socialists who were driving the country to rack and ruin. He was all for special-interest groups, depending on which ones, and he was solidly behind tax incentives for businessmen big and small because otherwise how could they expand and compete and offer more jobs and contain the *isms* of the world and thus make sure our children had the same high standard of living we were all enjoying?

That's what he was saying today, that last, and while Ella Mae had not heretofore thought much about it she could see it was important and every bit as essential as Jack Coombs said it was, so she stopped tasting her cabbage long enough to tell him that she and Edward agreed with him down the line and stood behind him one hundred percent.

"Now," Jack was saying, *"I leave you with my thought for the day. Ask not for whom the cash register rings, it rings for thee."*

"That's real nice, Jack," she told him. "I'll remember to tell that to Edward."

"Good day to all," Jack said, *"and a special Jack Coombs howdy-do to Wanda Lee Hummings of Route One, Salt Springs, celebrating her fifth birthday today. Many happy returns, Wanda."*

"The same goes here," Ella Mae said. Every day Jack Coombs finished up his editorial expression by wishing a child somewhere a happy birthday, and each time he did it a thrill went through Ella Mae. It made her feel good about being human. She thought it one of the nicest things imaginable.

Jack's five minutes were always up too fast. The regular announcer, with not nearly so good a voice, was reminding her now that editorial expressions taking a dissimilar opinion were invited and the station would be pleased to air them at a future date. As always, Ella Mae was intrigued by the absurdity of this offer. She couldn't see how anyone could possibly disagree with Jack Coombs, who had all the facts at his fingertips and proved beyond a shadow of a doubt everything he said in his editorial expressions. Happily, in two years she'd never heard a single person speak up with a dissimilar opinion. When Jack talked, she guessed, everybody else shut up. Edward said that was as it should be, you couldn't argue with the truth, even a fool knew that much. And Edward had put his finger on it, as usual, he'd hit the nail on the head.

Fred Joyner, when he was drinking, would sometimes go on about Jack Coombs, about how his voice was syndicated and how he had millionaire holdings in Eustacia and a dozen other places. Eula would jump in to say Jack Coombs was one of the biggest womanizers ever put

on green earth and that a teenage girl, she couldn't remember where, had won a court case against him over a
paternal question. "I just don't believe it," Ella Mae
would tell Eula. "You could tell me a cow has five legs
and a monkey can't climb trees and I would believe that
quicker."

"You're gullible," Eula would say. "You been stuck in
these woods so long your brain wears earmuffs."

Edward said that when you were on welfare like the
Joyners, and next door to being common drunkards, the
one thing you hated most was someone like Jack Coombs
coming along to rock the boat. She was proud of Edward, he didn't let those two get away with anything.

Hawaiian music had come on. Ella Mae took out her
hairpin and turned off the Philips. She personally liked
Hawaiian music fine, but she was rarely in a mood for it
after listening to Jack Coombs. Of course, Hawaiian
music was just what the doctor ordered once you were
ready to sit down and enjoy a hot dinner. In the old days,
when it came on half an hour later, they always listened
to it ("Amos and Andy" had come on just before, back
then), and Edward, if he was in a good mood—and the
boys too after they got over their natural shyness—would
get up and wiggle their hips like women, wiggle them
and roll their feet and let their hands flap up and down
just like Dorothy Lamour did in her movies.

Such good times, she thought now, sighing, heading
upstairs to make herself look pretty for Edward. Eating
high on the hog then, as her mama would say. She had
been slimmer then too, not slim but slimmer, and had
liked to look on the bright side. She had laughed and
laughed in those days, laughed to beat the band. Well,
once she caught Edward, she had. He'd be home, she
guessed, in about fifteen minutes—plenty of time to
wash her feet and put on a new face—and she reminded

herself to tell him what Jack Coombs had said today
about corporate tax relief being the answer to an ailing
economy because it was just what was needed to put the
little people back on their feet. She didn't understand it
exactly, but Edward would. He could maybe bring it
into play down at the yard, get all their troubles
straightened out, the nine or ten laid-off men could be
rehired, and maybe as a reward they'd give Edward a
desk with his name on it, as the Lord knew he deserved.
That was the trouble with people like her and Edward,
from the wrong side of the tracks, they were never given
a chance. She wished one day Jack Coombs would sink
his teeth into that fact the way he did unwed mothers
and abortions and smut magazines on the newsstands for
innocent children to look at.

If she had any complaint at all with Jack Coombs,
that would be it—he seemed to think everybody in the
world made fifteen or twenty thousand dollars a year like
him.

She turned on the tub tap, sprinkling Epsom salts in
the water. Her mama had sworn by Epsom salts, had
even used it when washing her hair. Her mama had
lovely hair down practically to her knees, though she had
always worn it up, tied so tight you'd swear she hardly
had hair at all. Well, styles change. And a farm woman
wouldn't be able to do her chores if she had hair swinging all over the place. It would catch fire every time you
lifted a stove lid, it would get caught in fences, and if you
were hoeing you wouldn't be able to see what you were
weeding. And, who knows, maybe some field hand would
come up behind you and catch you by it and just throw
you down.

An inch or so of water had run into the tub. She
grasped the towel bar and stepped carefully in, sitting
down on the cold lip, splashing water up around her

ankles while holding her dress up. She had lived with
these legs for years, she had had to carry them around,
but still she sometimes thought a mistake had been
made, that these legs were not her own. The skin was as
soft and beautiful as could be, up around the thighs, but
her hands would not go halfway around them. Edward,
feeling spiteful, would say one of her thighs was bigger
than his whole chest and had more hair on it too. Mean.
Why did people have to be so mean? She didn't go
around talking about people with hair in their ears or
warts in their eyebrows and she wished they'd show her
the same courtesy. No, they were always getting at you
over something and making it up when they couldn't
find it. Not all, but most. Yet Jesus had sat among the
lepers and he had let a common whore touch his rai-
ment. Suppose Jesus walked into her bathroom this minute. Would he say, Ella Mae your thighs are white as
cooked shrimp and they hang like a doorman's tummy?
No, he'd only calmly remind her that she was still
overeating and he hoped for improvement soon. He'd
tell her he knew she couldn't help herself. He'd tell her
he knew lots of women—and men too—with the same
problem and it wasn't so bad she ought to shoot herself.
And he'd find something nice to go along with his criti-
cism, on the order of *Ella Mae you have trim wonderful ankles
and I have never seen prettier feet on a woman.*

She pulled the plug and dried her feet where she sat.
She did have fine delicate feet—not a blessing exactly
since they so often hurt. As for size, she could probably
get both her feet into Eula Joyner's cowboy boots. And
while Eula was slim, she was no one's beauty. If Edward
flirted with her—and now and then he did—it was only
because he felt sorry for her.

Anyway, she thought, hanging up the towel, her
thighs were not fat, it was what they called cellulite and
even Elizabeth Taylor had it.

She remained seated, idly staring at the green plastic tile wall Edward had put up on his way to building a shower unit. He had run out of green and, against all her objections, had finished up with lavender ones that were not even the same size. He hadn't yet put in the shower head and the roughed-in (he called it) plumbing was there for everyone to see. It had been that way for two months now, postponed until he could find an elbow connection at a junk yard or stuck in a corner of somebody's garage. She had to admit it, that man was tight. He was so tight, Fred Joyner said, his shoes had to be screwed on.

There, of course, was one to talk.

Those two, Fred and Eula, were so tight they thought running water was something that happened when it rained. She remembered the time a VFW man had come on crutches and wearing two artificial limbs, soliciting for their Christmas drive, and Fred and Eula had stood out in their yard ordering him off their property, refusing to part with a dime. The paper boy, the same one who had been struck dumb seeing her on a ladder, had faithfully delivered them the *Clarion* every day except Sunday for three months, and she knew for a fact he was yet to get one red cent out of them. Every week or so the Credit Bureau man came and knocked on *her* door, wanting news of them. "They're home," she'd say, "far as I know." "Well, they won't come to the door," he'd reply. She'd ask who was after them this time, and he'd reel off a pack of names. She knew where they were, all right. With the dogs to warn them, no one could sneak up on the place, and they'd just hide under the bed until whoever it was left. When the city was putting in a water line, they'd refused to have anything to do with it once they learned they'd have to pay easement costs. So the sidewalk stopped, just as the city limits did, right where it met their property line. On hers and Edward's side of

the street, it went on down for another quarter mile, with
signposts to prove it.

It beat her how they got away with so much.

Yet here was Eula today talking about Edward's window bringing down their property value. What nerve.
True, they had a full acre, but she wouldn't give two
cents for it and everything on it.

Lord have mercy, she sud-
denly thought, here I am running everybody down, with
Edward due home any minute and me not even done my
face. She rolled off some tissue and wiped the medicine
cabinet mirror where the boys had splattered toothpaste.
None ever went into their mouths, it all went there. The
skin under her eyes was swollen from crying (she could
hear one of the boys wisecracking, "How can you tell?")
and she tried patting it smooth with a cotton ball
dabbed in Oil of Olay. She sprayed a generous cloud of
Evening in Paris behind her ears and over her throat.
She had hoped Edward would come up with Chanel No.
5 on her birthday, but as usual it was EIP again. She
wouldn't complain. It beat vanilla flavoring, which she
had been using when she met him.

She smeared lipstick—red but not too red—over her
bottom lip, smacked her lips together, and blotted. She
rubbed rouge into her cheeks, knowing Edward's prefer-
ence for a face with lots of color. She combed out her
hair, wishing she had a flower to put in it or at least a
bow, because Edward liked that. One of these days she
hoped to get herself a wig and false eyelashes and really
give him a surprise when he came through the door. She
had read in *Woman's Day*, and had herself observed, that

nothing drove a man to another woman quicker than having to come home every day to the same drab housewife and the same boring routine. On the other hand, two weeks ago she had painted on a black handlebar mustache with her mascara and not one of her three men had noticed. The next day she had moved Edward's recliner chair into the kitchen and told him to sit down, she had a surprise for him, and when she brought it he had said, "I don't want no water," and when she told him it wasn't water it was a martini, he had taken one sip and poured it down the sink and carried his chair back where he said it belonged. "You got strange ideas," he had said, "about what a man likes." That had hurt her so much she had gone out into the back yard to walk it off.

What would it be like, she asked herself now, heading back downstairs, to be married to a man like Jack Coombs whose voice went right through you to root you where you stood? She wasn't sure she'd like it, never knowing what idea he was going to throw at you next; living with him would be as bad as living with a preacher, in that respect. One thing for sure, his wife would never get any work done, too afraid she'd miss whatever word his silver tongue issued next. He wouldn't abide fools, that was obvious. Eula Joyner, for instance, she'd give Eula Joyner three days before he sent her packing. How about herself? A month, maybe two, assuming he wasn't prejudiced against large women or those who spoke their minds. Maybe a whole year if he liked good cooking, if he gave himself a chance to get to know her. If he didn't judge every woman by appearances. Of course, she thought laughing, I'd have to give up the children, my children, and give him three or four of his own. Anybody with a silver tongue like his was bound to have an appetite for sex.

Her biscuits were about ready, needing only a bit of

browning on top, the casserole was too, so she turned off
the oven, and put the smallest flame of gas under the
home fries and the cabbage to keep them warm. She expected to hear Edward's truck any minute. Usually, before he turned in the driveway, he quick turned the igni-
tion off and on to make the truck backfire and let her
know he was home. But he wasn't reliable, he'd forget
sometimes, so she usually stood by the front window
watching for him. She took up that position now, putting
off the time when she'd have to go out in the yard and
holler for the boys.

Now if Edward was a woman, him and Jack Coombs
would get along right from the start. Those two would be
as compatible as bees and honey. Sometimes she wished
Edward *was* a woman. At least a woman would talk to
you, you could sit down and have a serious chat with her,
she didn't run off every time you proposed it, saying she
had to "check the oil" or "square off a joint" or the hundred and one things Edward always said he had to do. If
Edward was a woman she could ask him what he had on
his mind by sealing up her bedroom window, and if he
was any kind of woman at all he would spell out his reasons, every one of them come what may, come hell or
high water.

She went back into the kitchen to check the time. He
was way late, she saw, and if he didn't show up soon her
dinner would be ruined. If he was a woman—well, a
woman would simply never pull such a thoughtless trick,
while men just thought food cooked itself and jumped up
on the table.

She began worrying about him, fearing a wreck, and
when next she went back to the window, she had two hot
buttered biscuits in her hands. She ate those quickly,
then returned for two more, telling herself she knew she
shouldn't but the fault was Edward's for getting her into

this state and if she put on a few more pounds he would just have to live with the blame. She rearranged the biscuits in the pan, knowing that he would count every one.

She went out into the yard and hollered for the boys. They didn't answer, though the Joyner dogs did. She stepped out to the sidewalk, looking, but saw no sign of them. Down the street a hundred yards or so was a car parked under the trees in the turnaround. She couldn't make out any heads, didn't have to because she knew well enough why they were there. They were having a drink. Ten or fifteen times a day, more on weekends, cars stopped there. Since it was beyond the city limits, the police could not do a thing about it except wait to see if they drove across the line drunk. The boys were always bringing home pint bottles they had picked up there, and once her youngest, Theodore, had come in stretching a filthy rubber thing between his hands, asking her to look at the good balloon he'd found. She'd turned red in the face and marched him straight up to the bath.

She kept calling. Her boys didn't appear.

The sky was thinning out, and the air had a bite to it. More than likely the ground would frost tonight. In another hour or so it would be getting dark; already the light had made that turn. It wasn't God's sky anymore. She had the feeling sometimes, had it now, that when God slept—or if He, out of stubbornness, just up and turned His back on the human race—the sky was left looking this way—cold and remote and so chillingly placid that all of it went inside you and made you want to cry or beat your head against the wall out of plain hopelessness.

Inside, she turned off her stove and, for company, got the Philips going. The Hawaiian Hour was over and the announcer was telling her to stay tuned for the community bulletin board. The First Baptist Church of New

Love was holding a bake sale Saturday at 2:00 p.m. and
Reverend T. T. Short, pastor, invited friends of all de-
nominations to attend. The Rod and Gun Club of Dry
Springs was having its usual Sunday turkey shoot at the
Atwood Farm out five miles east on Highway 48, with a
valuable raffle prize going to some lucky person. In
nearby Eustacia, the high school Thespian Society was
presenting, this week only, Wolfgang A. Mozart's light-
hearted musicale *Così fan tutte* in special English transla-
tion by well-known civic-woman Winnameer Riser.
The noted women's barbershop group The Fast Notes
would perform at intermission as an extra added attrac-
tion.

Ella Mae nodded to each of these, amazed as always
that so much was going on in her community. She marveled that people found time to do and see so much and
still take care of house and home. Every other week, for
instance, Winnameer Riser's name was mentioned; she
had done this or she had done that, she was ever up to
something. She was a big wheel at Eustacia Community
College, she was president of the Chess Club, she had got
a bookmobile program going and wanted something
done about stray animals, and last week her picture had
been in the paper with a write-up about her work with
the Nightingale Society, which did relief work in struggling nations not even Edward had ever heard of. A
pinch-faced, dopey-looking creature, you wouldn't think
she had a brain in her head. She was a little woman, not
more than five feet tall, yet as Edward had said, a man
would have his hands full trying to hold Winnameer
Riser down. She rode around nights in a police patrol
car, he said, and cussed like a sailor. Ella Mae admired a
woman like that, with energy to burn and nobody to be
responsible to, since apparently she wasn't married.
Imagine being Winnameer Riser! A woman like that

could get herself a man like Jack Coombs. You had to be Winnameer, with her get-up-and-go, to land a man like that.

Ella Mae had to face it; envy was what she felt these days anytime she heard Winnameer Riser's name. Where did such women come from? How did they acquire such confidence? What would it be like to go to bed every night satisfied that you'd done well and get up every morning knowing the new day would be even better? Not even in the bliss of her early days married to Edward had she ever known a similar contentment. Never in her childhood. Her daddy had said she was no-account. No more personality, he'd said, than an old rag or a lump of dough. Even her mama had called her a worrywart and a daydreamer. *Lord, child, if you don't move soon, the birds will come nest in your hair. You'll have spiders spinning webs from ear to ear.* Or the Jewel Tea man would drive up in the yard and tickle her under the chin, saying, "How's my little butterball? I bet you'd give me a kiss for one bite of my cakes." At school they'd call her Turnips. Fatso. Blimp. Lardo. How's the weather, they'd say, in that balloon? Winnameer Riser, she bet, had never had to put up with treatment like that. Winnameer Riser probably had everything handed to her on a platter, boyfriends who beat down her door, rides in open cars, dances, evenings with the moon cutting a silver path across a lake. A maid to give her hair one hundred strokes. Champagne in silver goblets, a father who smoked cigars while standing in his tuxedo by a roaring fire, violinists in the drawing room, carpets under her feet, and red roses spilling from a dozen vases. *Oh, do take away the vahzez, James.* Gowns hemmed with ermine, and at night a wide bed with satin to her neck. *Why, Mama honey, I'm so worried, I don't know which ball to go to next.*

She and Edward hadn't had balls to go to, or even a

moving picture show. They'd had RC colas to drink at a one-room country store, sitting on soft drink crates or upturned kegs of nails, eating pig's feet or pickled sausage from the brine of a gallon jug; and they'd had long walks down country roads with dogs sniffing at their heels. They'd had hills to sit on and corn rows to run through and creeks to wade in. They'd had morning glory vines and kudzu and honeysuckle and barns to hide behind if ever they had the wit or need or courage to be alone. Mostly they'd had his mama's kitchen to sit in, and church, when Edward was willing, and Sunday afternoons seated on rocks or stumps by the side of the road, a chew of twig in their mouths, benignly watching what little of the world there was that came their way. Mostly people you knew to speak to and trash you wouldn't want to speak to on a bet, and now and then, maybe twice on any given day, someone passing in a car you had never seen before, a salesman making his monthly or yearly rounds, or someone strayed off the main road, coming from and going to a place you never knew existed until he poked his head out the window and waved maps, asking how far and which way it was to whatever spot he thought was next. Edward liked directing people to a place. He liked telling them he'd seen the world, he'd seen Hong Kong and Manila and Borneo, he knew the China Sea like the back of his hand, he'd eaten a thousand coconuts off deserted islands in the Philippines, but now there wasn't one inch he'd swap of where he was for all of those places. No, he'd say, there wasn't enough money in the whole wide world to make him leave home again.

No one answered at the yard. She dialed Red Arrow's where Edward often stopped in for cigarettes or to chew the fat, but Red said he had not seen him today. She remembered that Edward liked to prowl the field at Sam Peabody Wrecks, but the man answering the phone told her Edward hadn't been around. She didn't know who else to try. Edward had so many friends, so many irons in the fire, she hardly knew where to start. Same with the boys. Frequently they complained they had no friends, nobody liked them, but she knew they were joking. High-spirited knockabouts like those two would never lack for friends. She went out in the front yard, once more yelling for them to come home; again only the Joyner hounds responded. She walked around the house and on down a footpath past the vacant lot where Earl Rice put in a crop of feed corn every season, along with several rows of greens, which either the drought got, or the weeds, or Eula Joyner once they came ripe for picking. She had seen her there more than once, in the dead of night, scurrying back across the street with her skirt full. A common thief. And naturally, Earl Rice would think it was her and Edward stripping his garden. Last summer he had appeared at her back door, a bent old man, eighty if he was a day, yellow pus running out of his eyes, asking if she'd seen anyone suspicious messing around.

"No, no," she said, her fingers crossed, "I haven't seen anyone." Blushing to tell such a plain-out lie, feeling such a rush of pity for that sick old man, who spent weeks on his knees, only to lose the fruits of his labor to

people like the Joyners who believed work was something that killed a body quicker than liquor could.

"You keep an eye out for me," the old man had said.
"It beats me how low-down some people are. I'd give the
shirt off my back to anyone in need, to anyone with the
good grace to ask. It's easy living that's done it. Folks
don't have the natural goodness they had in the old
days."

Amen, she could say, to every word of that.

Farther on down, where the path intersected with Pitts
Road leading out to Indian Mound, she stopped and
called again. She saw the boys nowhere, nor did they answer. The smell here was terrible—seepage from an old
septic tank, she thought. Puddles of oily sludge lay per-
manently about, tiny scraps of paper littering the
ground. The earth sucked at her heels, her own footprints filling up. Dwarf pines lined each side of the road.
Five miles down that road, Pitts Road, they'd dug up,
two years ago, an Indian burial mound, and she could
not look that way without being overwhelmed by an im-
mense sadness. They'd unearthed bones and pots made
from clay and Lord knows what else. A woman's skeleton
had been found bound up in skins and folded like a fetus;
inside the same pot with her were a dozen children's
skulls. Experts from the university said the bones had
been scraped. Other skeletons, men and women, had
been found buried in layers, down as far as ten feet, ex-
tending over an area roughly the size of a flatbed truck.
Maybe two thousand savages, they said, had lived there.
Yet they were a mystery. What tribe they were no one
knew and what had killed them off no one knew. From
their bones, one of the experts said, they could have been
as white as you or me. We could all, he seemed to be telling her, be bound up in skins and folded over in the
shape of an unborn child and put in the ground to rot

and be forgot. Ashes to ashes, dust to dust—here and gone. Ella Mae with her finger that ought to have been cut off and her feet flat from what they had to carry. Ella Mae with her children that wouldn't come home and her husband who had seen everything he wanted ever to see from their bedroom window—who wouldn't come home either. Life was just nothing at all. It had no more point to it than snakes in a basket. Bind her up in animal skin or burlap sack this very minute and drop her in an open pit and no one would care, no one mourn. Her own mama was gone and not a solitary person in the whole world, aside from herself, gave her a single thought. Being dead was an awful thing; even when life was nothing it seemed so. Her boys seeing her mama's picture in the family album, well, they could be looking at the moon for all the difference it made to them. "She looks a wiry old bird," Edward would say. "I never could figure how the watermelon comes off such a slender vine. Why, she don't look like she weighs eighty pounds!"

Her favorite photo was one of Mama standing outside on the kitchen steps holding a box of Jewel Tea in one hand and her broom in the other. The Jewel Tea man had taken it with his box camera. "One more satisfied customer," he had said, meaning to use the photo somehow, but he had not been able to talk Mama into putting down her broom, and after it was taken she had given the tea back to him, saying they couldn't afford anything just now, try her again maybe next month if he was coming round.

It was hopeless, life was, and sometimes when she was in this mood it made a kind of crazy sense to her how people like the Joyners were content to spend their lives doing nothing, drinking liquor, and crawling on their knees to bed every night. Likely as not her own two boys would grow up to marry women just like Eula Joyner, maybe without the cowboy boots, but like her just the same. And no doubt, if she was out of the picture, Edward himself would run out and pair up quick as he could with a real exciting woman, Winnameer Riser herself maybe, assuming the Jack Coombses in the world would let him have her. A thousand years from now when they dug Ella Mae up, that is if anyone thought it worth the trouble, folks would say, "Who was this fat ugly creature? Wonder what killed off this elephant?"

Even if she was able she wouldn't tell them. Shame wouldn't let her. She'd never be able to say, Well, it was because I never had nothing, never knew the joy of a loving home, the love of husband or children, it was because the whole wide world conspired to make me feel I was of no account and life wasn't worth living, it was these things that drove me headfirst into my grave.

Thinking of herself or Mama in the grave naturally made her thoughts turn to her daddy. To Poppa, though rarely had she felt close enough to him to call him that. Hard times had struck her mama down but Poppa had gone straight on living, if that's what you could call it when a person got his age and health had been thrown down the drain.

Poppa's brains now rattled around in his head like pennies in a teacup. Oftentimes he forgot where he was—though that hadn't stopped him from being mean.

Finally, last year she and Edward had put him in a rest home for his own good. For their own good too, as he had tried his level best to burn them out of house and home. The place would be in ashes now but for Theodore's good nose, thank the Lord.

He was at Bide-A-While home, not twenty miles away, like Edward said, getting meaner every day.

No one would ever know how much it had hurt her to

put him there, to walk him through the front door like
one would lead a child, with him pulling to go the other
way just like a child would and saying, "You ain't my
keeper, I ain't staying in this moldy place." *Moldy* being
just a word he used, because normally he'd as soon sit
down with a bunch of rats as sit with decent people. Sit
longer with rats, and seem to have more fun with them, if
you want to know the truth.

It had been an awful day. She had cried all the way
home, and had lain awake crying and telling Edward it
wasn't no one's fault, they had done what they had to do.

"We'll go and get him," Edward had said, "if that's
your likes."

She had felt guilty about it but it wasn't guilt altogether that had made her cry. She cried out of a sense of
woe, out of the recognition of something wrong having
gone on so long that nothing mortal man or woman did
now could set it right. Her grandparents, what little she
knew of them—and it seemed Family, what Family
meant, wasn't a thing in *her* family that folks felt a com-
pulsion to pass along—had known a life no better than
her mama and poppa knew, and those before them the
same or worse. *Dirt* people, they came up out of dirt and
it clung to them along with all the soil's rot, to the point
that she had come to believe that her ancestors, her family, hardly walked upright like good human beings but,
instead, *slid* where they went. They couldn't spell, they
couldn't do sums, history was nonsense that hadn't been
invented yet. It was as if they had come up out of the
sludge and blinked to find themselves in sunlight and
reached down to pick up a stick to hit at whoever was
standing nearest, and that had been the end of it, that
was as far as her family got, much as if God had not had
a solitary thing to do with it. Couldn't have had, least-
wise not a Christian God.

She had thought that with her getting the cream of the crop with Edward matters would change for her family, but she wasn't so sure anymore. It seemed to her that something, no telling what, was driving her and them all back into the dirt again and that it was this awful *something* that had got inside her to make her so big she had to turn sideways to get through a door that would hold ten Edwards stacked one upon the other and standing any way they pleased.

You struggled and you struggled and all for what. For children who behaved no better than wild beasts, and for a husband who boarded up your window and then wouldn't come home.

Lord, here I go, she thought, my thoughts run like honeysuckle on a wire fence. Start off getting miserable about Poppa and two seconds later I'm running down my own two sweet boys and giving in to pity for myself. If Jesus was here beside me now, he'd take a switch to me, he'd say, Woman open your eyes, I offer the path of truth and light but until your head is held high you will never see it. You have not visited your own daddy at Bide-A-While in near a month, woe unto you, for although he is a sinner he is as precious to me as the shorn lamb, and I would remind you what happened to the Pharisees when they set themselves up to judge. Judge not that ye be not judged, or suffer eternal fire, as my servant Eelbone has told you until he's gone blue in the face.

She put out a hand. The words were in her own head, though she knew Jesus had put them there, that he was near. She felt calm again, and there was nothing so miraculous about it, it was just God's way. All things were possible if you gave your hand to Jesus. The sick would take up their beds and walk and the fat would be made slim. Tomorrow, she vowed, she would not touch a cookie all day and Dairy Queen could go broke before she'd pass them another dime. If every time she put out a hand to lift another biscuit to her mouth she had instead put her hand in his, she would be as lean as Bette Wiffle today, she wouldn't ever again suffer these gravedigger doubts.

"I'll go see Poppa," she told herself. "I'll have Edward drive me out this very weekend. I'll make it up to Eula with good deeds or you can pour salt in my mouth. I'll stop sleeping in the daytime, which is one of the worst evils known to man. I'll be a good mother and the finest wife any man could desire."

She went on speaking thus, and although she meant every word, she was aware that she'd made this same speech many times before and that this time something crucial was missing, the edge had worn off and her soul was down to bone, like lead showing up under brass that had seen the polishing cloth too often.

She needed reviving, a revival of feeling, and not even Jesus standing nearby could do it. She didn't want to visit her daddy, for instance, wanted never to set eyes on him again and she might as well admit to it. Poppa hated her, that is if you could hate a body you'd spent your life ignoring in the first place, and for her part, she had no respect for him, she'd sooner claim as her parent the ugliest monkey in the zoo. She'd see him and he'd leave her feeling so sick and wrung out she'd have to ask for Edward's help to get herself back to the truck and home again. No, it wasn't even Poppa, come to think of it, it was what he stood for, him and Eula and Fred and what she feared would soon describe her own life as well: the senselessness, the no-accountness, the long, boring, impoverished wastefulness, waste so thick inside yourself sometimes you felt you could ladle it out with a spoon. And all the time you ladled, you knew you were only tak-

ing skim off the top, that the task was futile, be better off
trying to empty a flooded boat on the open sea.

The view was horrible, and she hid her face in her
hands out of shame that the view was accurate and true
and unpardonably her own.

In the distance she could see the backside of her own
house and the concrete blocks Edward had dumped
there two years ago, meaning to put in a barbecue pit,
but the sight of home afforded her no joy. It mystified
her that this should be so, for she had started out in that
house with such hopes. Theirs had been but a two-dollar
wedding, with an imbecile woman brought in to serve as
witness from where she'd been on her knees cleaning up
the toilets at Eustacia's city hall, but Ella Mae had been
convinced she and Edward were off to a good start in
climbing the ladder of success; they were saying in coming to this house in a good-sized and growing town that
they were as good as people would let them be and that
they hereby renounced the slug life that had been theirs
up to then. But time and chance had got away from
them, somewhere along the line they'd slid back into the
mud. Once she had thought of this house as pretty, as a
cut above others in the neighborhood; now she acknowledged that it possessed no special claim of beauty or
meaning, it was just something stuck up on the land
without any thought of being in harmony with where it
was stuck, with hope only that it wouldn't fall down in
the first high wind. What it was a cut above, perhaps,
was the cave they might have found themselves living in
a thousand years before—or they might have wrapped
animal skins around three long poles the way the Indians
at the Mound were said to have done. She might as well
shoot herself now, and Edward and the boys into the
bargain, for all that house amounted to. It was empty,
empty and ugly and stood for nothing, and to her mind

there was no telling how long this had been so. The field she was this minute passing through was all rubble and swamp and moldy growth; it had been cleared at one time of all except stumps and boulders too big even for a team of mules to pull, but now, as quickly as the sour air would allow, it was going back to nature, being claimed by and for the devil's own, just as was the case with her and Edward and their soulless marriage.

I've come up out of mud to walk life's darkest road, she thought, with no moon to guide me and only briar and brush swishing at my ankles to let me know what road I was on. I've tried to raise myself up bootstrapwise, the way a caught rabbit, squirrel, or coon will chew off limbs to get the trap off him. Now I've come to this. A mud rat knows water that is his own, and I guess not knowing mine was my big mistake—thinking mud was not good enough for me and not where I belonged. All the time I thought I was shedding mud, I've only been slapping more of it on. I have chewed one leg off and thought to escape but I should have kept on chewing till both me and trap were gone. Now I've come to this.

People do rise up, I know that. They do. But not us. What sense we've had we could have poured out of a boot for all the good it's done us. Yet people can rise up. Girls with mud squishing between their toes have put on shoes and waltzed into a new life. Boys with their britches held up by baling wire, they've put on a necktie and made the grade. I could call the roster of them—could but won't, because what's the use? Esselee Pardee, half Indian and my age at Gaston School, once upon a time was nothing, just like me. To mention one. Spit curls in our hair and our stomachs growling when we stood to recite our ABC's. Esselee Pardee now lives, I'm told, in a smart house on a high hill and owns in her name everything her eye can see from whatever stump she thinks to stand on. Beholden to no one and going her own way.

Oh, it can be done. But not by us. Not by me, anyhow. I'd be best off dropping down dead right here.

A door slammed shut, off in the distance somewhere. Then she saw movement at her kitchen window and Edward's truck in the driveway and her heart immediately lifted, her face lit up into a full smile, and she took off running; no, not running, she could not exactly run, but she brought one arm up quickly to her chest and with the other more or less shoved herself along, stumbling, her feet squishing through the muck, thinking, *Ella Mae, you are vile, you are beneath contempt. God ought to reach down and choke you with His very own hands,* but happy now, grinning ear to ear, meaning none of it as the distance closed between her and home, between her and Edward and all she prized in the live-long world.

Edward looked up from his bent position at the stove—he'd been sniffing at her pots, she noticed that—as the back door slammed and she rushed inside.

"Whoa, now!" he said.

She groped past him for a chair, unable just yet to speak, her breath short, her skin hot and perspiry.

"You look like you been chased by the devil's own ghost," he observed cheerily. "The four-minute mile already been broke." His voice had that singsongy high pitch it took on whenever he was especially pleased with himself. He moved in her direction, springy on his heels; she pulled her legs up under the chair to hide her soggy shoes. His rough hand fell lightly on her brow. With his thumb, he peeled back her left eyelid. "You'll live though. You got good focus. They tell me when a body dies or is about to, the eyeballs roll up inside the head—looking for heaven is my guess." He let out a cackle, then stooped, giving a quick peck to her cheek.

Lo and behold, she thought, lo and behold! If I wasn't sitting, I'd be falling down. She could count on two hands the months that had gone by since he'd given her one of his kisses of his own free will. Now, Edward in his prime had been quite the romancer. She'd seen women turn scarlet from no more than a flutter of his lashes.

He backed up, grinning broadly, turning to show off his clothes. Clearly he was in one of his rare moods. He had taken off his overalls and put on his new gabardines (well, new three years ago) and his pink Arrow shirt with the button-down collar. He had on his wide belt with the shiny buckle that read DRINK RED ROCK COLA. He had shaved and splashed on a handful of Old Spice. Tiny tears of toilet paper, held on by dots of dry blood, were scattered over neck and chin where he'd cut himself.

"Admit it if you want to," he taunted. "The person sharper than yours truly ain't yet been born!"

She loved it. She could go on till doomsday watching Edward when he was in his good mood. Now, tonight, right this minute, he didn't look a day older than he did the day she married him. And what he said was true: Edward dressed up was pretty as a thousand-dollar bill.

She got claim on her voice and spoke petulantly, remembering her earlier vexation: "Supper's mostly ruined. Where you been?"

"Been right here waiting for you. I had time to spic and span myself"—he dipped in front of her to show the neck he'd scrubbed—"and to worry if some fella hadn't run off with you."

"Shoot!" she laughed, slapping her thighs.

"Shoot fire and save matches," he added, an old joke he'd been repeating since they were kids.

She sat marveling at this new Edward. Her Redeemed Edward, almost her Born Again Edward. A cut-up from the word go. God Himself, she reflected, wouldn't be able to stay mad at him for more than a minute.

"I see you got the table laid out pretty as a picture. I bet not even the Queen of Hispopatania sets a fancier table." Hispopatania was the land Edward had invented for where no one ever had to do any work and could walk about every day in satin shoes.

"Oh, Edward," she gushed, "what's come over you?"

"Nothing you can't cure." He gave a licentious wiggle of his hips. He scratched a match against his rear end, lighting up one of his Camels. "Watch this." He took a puff on the cigarette, dropping his head far down into his shoulders. He made hocus-pocus motions with his hands. When next his head shot up, the cigarette was protruding from one ear.

Learned it in the Navy, he'd say.

"You been drinking, Edward? I bet you stopped off and had yourself one."

"Not me. I'm dry as an undertaker's tears."

He removed the cigarette, hid it with a roll of both hands, then upended his empty palms inches from her face. "Geronimo!" he cried, spreading both arms wide. The cigarette was now dangling from his nose. He inhaled and smoke streamed out of the empty nostril.

She whooped with delight. Edward with a cigarette was more fun than Liberace on a piano stool. She never had been able to understand, and couldn't now, why no-talent people, like for instance Johnny Carson, could make a million dollars swinging at a golf ball that wasn't there, while her Edward, the funniest man alive, had to root out a living in a freight yard.

"I thank you kindly," he intoned, bowing.

She hefted herself up, intending to hug him.

"Don't wrinkle the merchandise," he laughed.

He made as if his bones were popping as her arms encircled him. "Sold!" he cried, wheezing, "to the woman with the purple finger. Going going gone!"

She let him go; he tumbled to the floor, limp as a dishrag. She crossed to the stove, remarking that there was work to do, she had no more time for his foolishness.

He clambered to his knees, barking like a dog. He crawled between her legs, taking nips from her ankles. Then he started growling and biting in earnest.

"Now stop that, Edward," she giggled, swatting at his head with a potholder. He stopped at once. She went on with her work. When she next looked he was on his back on the floor, his arms and knees held high and bent like four paws, tongue lolling from his mouth.

"Land-sakes, Edward, you don't have the sense you were born with."

He remained where he was, panting and twitching now, looking for all the world as if he were at death's door except for the single eye which opened to stare at her. She felt a rush of love, of desire, so tender and powerful that she had to close her eyes, to suck in and hold her breath. It was all she could do to keep herself from dropping down on top of him and letting him take her then and there.

He took to making little puppy whines. He rolled slowly up on hands and knees and, crawling, whining, came up under her dress. His tongue licked at her thighs. He licked, and went on licking and whining. She felt on the edge of a faint and leaned back against the refrigerator, holding on tight. She squeezed her legs together but his head was like a smooth though bristly thing and kept on sliding through to some new place his tongue had not stopped at before.

She was in his power. Edward Hopkins can do anything in the world he wants to do with me, she thought.
I'm but a puppet in the Master's hands.

TV noise from the living room, laughter that Edward
claimed came in cans, brought her to her senses. She
shoved down her dress, scrambling away. "Is that the
boys? Are they home? I called and called but those
scamps wouldn't come."

Edward got up. He had a sheepish look and she could
tell he was surprised at himself.

"They're home now is all I know. Watching 'Hee
Haw.' That channel from Eustacia is coming in clear as
a bell since I rewired the set."

She went in to check for herself. The boys were seated
together in the recliner pulled up about one foot from
the TV screen, gray light flickering over them.

"How you boys doing?" she asked from the door.

Little Theodore wiped his nose on his sleeve; they continued to stare intently at the screen.

"You boys hungry? Didn't you hear me calling you a
while ago?"

Ike darted out on an arm, turned the TV volume
higher.

"Well, move that TV back some," she said in her
threatening voice. "You know you can get poisoned from
sitting too close." She waited. They looked neither at
each other nor at her. Their expressions didn't alter as
Fat Edna, or whatever was her name, stood in the familiar cornfield telling a joke about the traveling salesman
who had followed her there. An arm reached up and
yanked her down. A second later a pair of wide red
bloomers came sailing up above the corn. A few more
seconds passed before six or seven other bloomers were
pitched up from other rows. TV laughter erupted, and
she saw Ike nudge Theodore soberly in the ribs.

8 5

"Dinner in a minute," Ella Mae told them. "Mind you wash your hands."

Buck Owens came on, saying he would like now to sing his new hit song. *"If you hit it I'll cook it,"* Grandpa Jones said. The whole gang laughed.

"Those boys," she sighed, coming back into the kitchen, "are going to be my death."

"Nothing wrong with them," replied Edward good-naturedly, "that a thrashing now and then won't cure." He was running the prongs of her fork up under his nails. Tiny balls of dirt were scattered over her china plate. She smacked at his hands, lifting the plate away.

"You hungry?"

"Stomach rubbing backbone," he said.

She began transferring food to the table.

"How was work?"

"Fine. Nothing new."

"Pretty busy, eh?"

"So-so. About the same."

She settled a bowl of cabbage under his nose. He picked out a forkful and put it in his mouth. "Now that's cabbage," he said, chewing.

"How's your bossman Mr. Hargroves doing? You and him getting along okay?"

"Thick as thieves. Why you ask?"

"Just wondering. What's wrong with his throat? You told me but I forgot."

"He's got a yardstick stuck up in it, that's what's wrong with Hargroves. You ask me, he ought to have something stuck up somewheres else."

She called to the boys. She kept on bringing food to the table. Edward would take a nibble of each dish as she put it down, and nod his approval or not nod. She watched him closely, pretending not to, for the Lord knew Edward was a touchy eater. Eating, Edward was a puzzle to her. Most times he didn't eat enough to keep a tick alive.

"I hear they're laying off men down at the yard."

"Yep." He had split the top off a biscuit and was biting into it, but paused, studying her. "You hear that on the radio?"

"Just before Jack Coombs. They already laid off eight or ten, so the news said, and more to come. You worried any?"

"Not me."

"Mr. Hargroves called. He wants to see you first thing tomorrow."

"Is that a fact?"

She nodded.

"Well, he can take a flying leap."

"I hear the yard might even shut down. I don't know what we'd do if that happened, do you?"

He didn't answer.

"I'd sure hate to go on relief like Eula and Fred. They'd never let us hear the last of it."

He got up and left the kitchen, scowling, going in to round up and herd in the boys.

He's worried, she thought. That man is upset and concerned for what will happen to me and the boys. If he gets fired or laid off, he won't be able to hold his head up in this town. They had might just as well shoot him between the eyes and be done with it.

Supper didn't go well.

The boys got into a squabble over who hated every mouthful the most.

"This here cabbage stinks," Ike said.

"Mine's rotten," Theodore chimed.

"This here cabbage got worms," Ike said. "I got me a whole plateful of worms and spiders and maggots and it all stinks and I hate it."

They were peas in a pod, those two, and they were driving her to distraction. She looked to Edward to say something to them, but he just sat there grinning as if he thought them the two brightest, most delightful children ever.

"Muck, that's what it is," Ike said. "This muck stinks." He had shoved all his food in a circle around the edge of the plate. Each time he used his fork, more fell off. Food formed a ring completely around his plate. He began scooping it all together in a pile.

Theodore was pulling his into his lap and from there spooning it in big globs to the floor. "Slop," he said. "Wormy, mushy slop."

Ella Mae sat with clenched teeth, wanting to slap the three of them. She didn't yet say anything. She wanted to see for herself how much Edward let them get away with before he stopped grinning and reached over to shake the daylights out of them.

He wasn't eating, either. He would take a tiny mouthful, then he would drag on his cigarette; then he would put the cigarette back in the ashtray, watch it burn for a while, then take another tiny mouthful. He refused to take the pretty folded-up napkin off the table and put it in his lap like anyone with common sense would do.

"How else you going to get the grease off your lips? You don't see any grease on my lips, do you?" She patted her lips with her own napkin, as if to show him how. "I declare, Edward, there are times when you act like you just stepped off the boat."

He grunted. That was as much as she could get out of him. Just grunts and the occasional "uh" and now and again his smoke blowing across her face. He seemed to

have used up all of his good mood. It seemed to her that
he wasn't even trying.

"Has the cat got your tongue?" she asked, making an
effort to hide her irritation. "Don't you have *nothing* to
talk to me about?"

He shrugged.

Theodore suddenly began bawling, whining that Ike
was kicking him under the table.

"He kicked me first!" Ike shouted back. "The little
runt, I ought to kill him!"

They were both screaming now, grappling at each
other as they dived under the table.

"Your daddy is going to make you stand in the corner
if you don't behave! Come out of there this instant, you
hear me? He is going to blister your behinds good. Aren't
you, Edward?"

But Edward was in dreamland, not paying them or
her the slightest attention. He had folded up the aluminum foil from his cigarette package and was now picking
his teeth with the edge. There were perfectly good tooth-
picks in a glass right in front of him but, no, he couldn't
bother to use any of the tools God intended for the pur-
pose. She glared at him, telling herself that he was the
one responsible, that it was his leniency and weak backbone that had turned Ike and Theodore into little
hellers. They were down there now, scooting between her
legs, kicking and punching and setting up a caterwaul to
make her head ring.

"Now quit! Quit, I say!"

But they went right on. Oh, they'd go right on until
their jaws were wired or until a body had to pick up a
hammer and hit them between the eyes with it.

She felt tears sliding down her cheeks. All day I'm in
this house by my lonesome, she thought, looking forward
to a happy family reunion, the one hour in the day when
we can sit down together and show each other a little

human love. But every day it is the same. I find myself in the company of two hyenas and a lamp post.

She spooned more food onto her plate. The plate was empty and she couldn't imagine where her first serving had gone.

She caught Edward's eye, and although she knew the catching was accidental on his part, her face instantly brightened. "Is your tea sweet enough?" she asked.

"It's plenty sweet, thank you."

That made her smile. When he wanted to, Edward had such a nice way of talking, almost fancy, like an actor in a movie. "Jack Coombs says the country is going to rack and ruin," she pronounced gaily, "and it's all on account of business can't make a fair profit because everywhere you look it's union, union, union and people saying gimme, gimme, gimme! Polecats, he says they are."

That didn't get a rise out of him, his gaze traveling from her to the wall to his yellow fingernails.

"Eula paid a visit!"

The boys peeped up at her over the table edge, like those old drawings painted on walls that said KILROY WAS HERE. Their faces were blue, their eyes popping, each trying to see who could hold his breath longer.

Jesus save them.

"Fred was in bed. Sleeping off another drunk is my guess. His liver is going to kill him one of these days. I bet that man has bedsores on his backside big enough to point a stick at."

Nothing. She'd have been better off trying to strike up a conversation with an Indian or a dead man. She swallowed, swirled another chunk of potato into gravy, and kept going: "Winnameer Riser's got another big musical evening coming up over Eustacia way. I sure would like to hear her sometime. They say she sings real good."

Most days that remark would have pried loose his

tongue. Edward had the notion that women's voice boxes were cut wrong for either singing or talking— "Pinched in the joists," he'd say—never mind that her own voice was deeper than his. But not today. He was pulling nails and bolts and screws from his pockets and counting them in one palm like change.

"Well, that's all my news!" she now cried, throwing up her hands and laughing. "Everything else is right there for you to read in your paper!" She thumped her chest several times, broke off another biscuit, and reached for her iced tea. Her plate was empty again, Lord knows how.

I'll have just a teensy bit more, she told herself, and then quit, no need of making a pig of myself.

Her sore finger was throbbing. She could feel its heat through her dress. The finger was about the ugliest thing she'd ever seen on a human being and it made her sick to look at it. She groaned involuntarily. Edward didn't notice or seemed not to, and the boys were down flat on the floor, unmoving, pretending that something—her dinner no doubt—had killed them.

Edward lit up another Camel and reached for the paper. He'd been smoking since he was seven years old, so he had once told her, and if today he had all the money he'd spent on the weed, he'd be sitting pretty and be about eight feet tall. He had little ash worms all down the front of his shirt.

"Finger bothering you any?" he asked.

"Oh no," she quickly replied, "it feels fine!"

"Stubborn as a mule," he glared. "Beats me why you won't have it tended to."

She hid it in her lap, rounding her shoulders and drawing into herself. *If thy eye offend thee,* she felt he was saying, *then pluck it out.*

"I'm scared. I know they will take one look and chop it off."

"You're going to lose the whole arm, you don't watch out. Your wrist is already swole up big as a Christmas turkey."

It was true. Her wrist and the entire hand were enormous. The swelling went all the way up to her elbow. The skin was beet red.

"It's hot as a wood stove, I bet. I bet all day you been gritting your teeth from the pain."

The boys clambered up to have a good look, poking and pulling and falling all over each other. She whimpered, rocking forward with closed eyes, wishing she could set herself inside a box and close the lid. The pain from her finger was nothing compared to what she felt from Edward's harping. It was like God Himself was shaking a stick at her and saying *Ella Mae Hopkins, account for yourself! Ella Mae Hopkins, you are just no good! Ella Mae Hopkins, you vex me something awful!*

"They can drain that there finger, you know. They can suck out the rancid poison. I reckon if they can cut a Siamese twin in half or put in artificial kidneys like they going to have to do with Fred Joyner, they can fix up your poor finger."

They will cut off my whole arm, she thought. I'll be an amputee and Edward will leave me because he won't put up with no one-arm woman anymore than he would put up with a woman with a filthy mouth or one who lets hair grow in her armpits.

"Mama's crying," her little boy said. He sounded so pathetic and forlorn and sorry for her that she was close to reaching out and hugging him for the comfort only a child can give, but before she could move he was singing, "Crybaby, crybaby, stick your finger in your eye, baby!" and going "Yah-yah!" and she wanted to smack his face, and would have, had she the strength.

The room went silent and for some seconds all she heard was her own dry sobbing, and a *tick-tock tick-tock* from somewhere in the room. She peeped out between her fingers and there was Edward with the newspaper spread out over her dishes, and on the paper the black, beat-up Baby Ben that he'd put in a closet six months to a year back, saying one day he'd have it working again like new.

"There, that'll do it!" he said, and slammed it down in front of him beside his pocketknife screwdriver. He slid it over for her to take a look at, and the instant she picked the clock up, curious herself to see what time it was, it stopped ticking. It rested cold in her hand like a time bomb you couldn't hear, the glow-in-the-dark hands pointed straight up to twelve noon like he had meant for her to know what time it was in China or Australia or some other far place.

He wasn't noticing. He had fixed it or thought he had and was now unconcernedly scanning the *Clarion* front page, going from the weather forecast in the top right corner (no rain and none coming) to today's Funny Bones quote in the top left corner and finally dropping to the headline YARD LAYOFF LOOMS, his face darkening. He said something under his breath that she couldn't quite hear. Probably it had to do with the picture of Mr. Hargroves with a cigar in his mouth and a yardstick stuck up his you-know-what.

"You want more iced tea, Edward?" she asked. "I know how you dote on iced tea once the decent weather sets in."

He grunted, and she poured, looking over the top of his thinning hair at some movement in the far corner that had caught her eye. A rat maybe, though Edward claimed there were no rats in this house, only mice. And mice wouldn't hurt you, so what was the use of worrying? But it was rats, big enough to haul off a baby, and she had seen them. Nothing was there now, however, except dust and cobwebs, and that was enough to shame her.

She shivered, remembering an evening in her childhood when a rat had come up on her bed to chew at the bedpost and how it had gone right on chewing even after she had shrieked and thrown a shoe at it.

Her daddy had said rats proved there was life around a place.

The need for close human warmth came over her so suddenly and with such violence that she did not think to resist it. She grabbed Edward behind the head and yanked his face firmly against her bosom, holding him against her, her head swimming, through the few brief seconds before he broke free, kicking and squirming.

"You gone crazy!" he yelled, red with embarrassment.

She eased herself back down into her chair, avoiding his furious stare, embarrassed herself because she knew it was a sin to vaunt one's affection in front of innocent children. Ike stood picking his nose, looking at nothing, but Theodore was hanging in the doorway, examining her with the special contempt he reserved for women who couldn't keep their hands to themselves.

The table needed clearing, dishes needed doing; she couldn't bring herself just yet to launch into the task. For all that her menfolks minded, she could have put a Swanson's TV dinner in front of them and saved herself the trouble. The newspaper rustled, Edward snorting as he followed his finger down the few inches of the Lost & Found column. He never lost anything himself but was always looking for what other people might lose or turn up, reckoning, she supposed, that it would somehow eventually wind up in his hands.

She eyed the succotash bowl. Did she want more of that, or did she want the sweet peas, or should she save space for the custard pie in the refrigerator from yesterday, assuming it hadn't been finished off? "Look at me," she laughed. "With all this talking about hurt fingers, I hardly have had time to eat a mouthful."

Edward was reared back in his chair, scratching at his neck with one hand like he had fleas and writing figures on the newspaper with the other. He didn't look up. She pulled the succotash bowl over.

He let her have four or five spoonfuls before speaking up: "Have all you want! No sir, their ain't no war on. If that don't do you, I reckon me and the boys be willing to stir something else up!" He slapped the table with the flat of both hands, guffawing at his own joke. Behind her, the boys snickered.

"She eat any more, she will pop!" crowed Theodore.

They approached her elbows and stood by, watching.

There was the faint smell of pee on one of them.

She noticed Ike's eyes rolling in his head and knew he was trying to think of something smart-alecky to say. So she was ready to swat at him when he finally said, "I reckon you weigh more than the whole house, Mama." But she didn't swat. She pushed the bowl back and lowered her head.

"More than the moon, I'd say," Theodore amended.

"More than a tree."

"Or a boxcar or a dump truck."

"Now, now, she don't weigh that much." It was Edward who said this, smiling along with their giggles. "You boys calm down. You don't want to hurt your mama's feelings."

She had pulled the tablecloth up to hide her face.

"What did I tell you," Edward went on, "you have made her cry."

Ike crept in to peek at her face. She stomped hard at his foot, and he reeled back. "Nobody in this house loves me," she sobbed. "None of you have the feelings of a dirt dauber. You'd like nothing better than to see me dead."

"It would take a big hole," observed Theodore. "Maybe the whole graveyard."

She heard Edward howl and came out from under the tablecloth to shoot daggers at him, sitting there beaming like he'd just laid a golden egg. Him with his stained teeth and skinny as a beanpost, but did she ever throw that up to his face? No, she prided herself on showing a little common decency to her fellowman and not always turning the knife in where they hurt most and where they couldn't help themselves. *Cast ye not the first stone else ye be hit between the eyes,* as Preacher Eelbone said. But she was in for it, and knew it. They would go on taunting her tonight until the roof caved in.

The bowl of succotash was in her lap and the spoon in her hand. She looked at both, unable to think how they'd come to be there.

"Ain't missed a beat," cackled Edward. "If a cyclone come through here, I bet it wouldn't slow you down one iota."

She could feel her hackles rising. If ever I'm going to hit that man, she thought, now's the time. He didn't look like her husband anyway, but like some ugly scarecrow someone meant to fool her with. Suddenly, she found her voice: "I can eat all I want!" she shouted. "I can keep on stuffing my mouth until I'm big as a tank or I can slim down skinny as Cinderella and it wouldn't make any difference in the way I'm treated around here! I'd be dog-in-the-manger whatever my size." She jabbed at Edward with the spoon, and went on doing so as the bowl overturned and dropped its puddle in her lap. "If you want me to pack my bags, I'll go and pack them! If it hurts your eyes to look at me, just tell me and I'll be on my way before you can say scat! I'll not stay a minute more than I'm wanted!"

Ella Mae's eyes were screwed tight as they would go. It was as if the world's strongest man had his thumbs pressed into her sockets, bearing down for all he was worth. The bowl clattered to the floor; she rocked with its momentum, moaning, hands clenched together as one fist between her legs. Her head throbbed with pain, scalp stretched so taut she feared skin would burst and her brains pour out. Pain lifted her out of the chair. She could feel her feet swinging free in space. The chair fell away, yet still she hung, twisting, kicking her legs to find the floor. She became aware of something else: the room was getting smaller. She kicked faster, frightened, her breath coming in gasps, as the walls closed upon her. No, not the walls; it was her own body enlarging by the second. She tried to scream, to call Edward's name. But her mouth was enormous, cavernous. Sound had no place to go. Now her lips were closing up tight, an opening scarcely larger than a pinhead, her cheeks ballooning. The pain altered inside her head; she understood that her eyes had been pressed through to the back of her skull, and she opened them, amazed at what she saw. She was looking down into her own raw insides, into the giant trough which served as the stomach of a creature whose only pleasure was to eat. Rank fumes drifted up in waves of stench, as if from a seething pool of rot and filth. She could discern small boiling pockets, eruptions. The fumes momentarily parted. Down there to the left lay a bed of cabbage, leaves scarcely chewed, bacon strips still intact. Potatoes had rolled every which way. Unidentifiable meats churned in a slick puddle at the center; there were the beans and corn and the biscuits marked where her teeth had bitten into them. The odd bone or cut of fat shot to the surface and was instantly snatched down again. Pockets of sugar, inert, lay all around. Ringing her stomach lining was a doughy mess that looked like the cookies she had eaten today. Small rivers of grease formed, then vanished, to appear a second later elsewhere. The entire putrid mass churned at a slow boil, scummy little bubbles collecting on top. Revolting. How could a child of God pile in so much?

She gave a sudden involuntary cry. Something quaked in her, something was alive down there. Some gigantic beast stirring from her depths, rising. The sludge darkened, the foul air thickened. The stench was incredible, wave after wave of it and worsening by the moment, fanned apparently by this new turbulence. The sludge hissed, spreading outward from the center in furrows that folded one upon the other, their force building, now smashing with an acidic burn against her stomach wall. She could see the creature's form just below the surface now, moving quickly, changing direction at will, narrow and long and ugly as a crocodile. At once, the festering bog exploded, spray shot up to scald her throat. She looked on, transfixed, horrified, as the huge Stomach Serpent roared to the surface. It was hideous, stunning in its ugliness. It had eyes exactly like her own, although a thousand times larger, the lids crusted with knotty swirls of decay, carpets of fecal matter. Odious, an appalling sight. The horrible eyes stared momentarily into her own, without meanness or threat, entreating only, then they closed and the serpent's great mouth slowly opened. The jaws were rhinoceros jaws, terrifying; the mouth opened and kept on opening, massive, filling the enormous pit that was her stomach until mouth was all there was: black vast hole, darkness without end, commanding *Feed me! Feed me! Feed me!*

Normal silverware was absurd, a mockery. Her bones knocked with hunger, greed swept through her. She must appease this monster, fill and close that cavernous mouth, satisfy that groaning benign serpent, which was as helpless as she was herself. She must rake food in with both hands, pack it down; taste was not an issue, one's

dignity was no match for such hunger. Let the world go
on with its ignorant derision, its obscene jokes, what did
the world know!

She tried to lift her arms but someone, something, was
holding them down. She yanked. The grasp was firm; she
was held tight. Tied down. She could not move. "Stop
your fretting," she heard someone nearby shout. "Be
herself in a minute." Something cold and wet was
slapped on her brow. Rivulets washed down her cheeks.
"Having one of her spells! Stop fretting, I told you!" She
recognized the voice: Edward's. Precious Edward, she
thought, why is he tending me? And was surprised to
find his face a foot away, sideways, peering into hers with
alarm. His hand flapped in front of her eyes. She
blinked, sought to slap that hand away, but couldn't.
Hers were still tied down. "Bring another cloth," she
heard him say. There was Ike behind Edward, looking
frightened. His face was dirty from playing; she'd not
noticed that earlier. "Mama's having a fit," he said. Edward peeled the wet cloth from her brow, touched it to
the inside of his wrist, nodded, and slapped it back.
"Your mama don't have fits," he told Ike. Theodore approached, grinning, tongue hanging from his mouth, his
head rolling. "I can have fits too," he said. "I can have
good fits." Ike laughed.

"Your mama don't have fits," Edward repeated.
"Hush your mouths." Again he peered at her. It seemed
to Ella Mae that his face made a soft smile.

"Loose my arms, Edward," she begged. "You got no
cause to hog-tie me."

"The joke's on you, Ella Mae," he said.

And it was true. She lifted her arms as easily as she
ever could. Nothing at all, unless it was the devil, had
been holding them down.

Edward pulled up a chair. "Put your feet up. You
done gone and blacked out on us, near as I could tell. Put
your feet up, relax a spell." He lifted her legs, lowered

her heels into the chair. "There now. How's that? You're as comfortable as any rich woman. Had us half out of our wits, I don't mind telling you." He put spit on his fingertips and smoothed down something on her head.

They formed a partial circle around her. Little Theodore's eyes were wet; he was fidgeting as if he had to do his business. Her family. Her sweet ragamuffin boys, near enough alike as twins, and Edward, good as any doctor. She longed to reach out and hug them, tell them all they meant to her. *You're mine, and I couldn't survive a day without the three of you. You're all that I have between me and wishing my daddy had put me in a tow sack and chucked me into a creek. My pride and joy. I am blessed,* she thought. *I am truly blessed, Lord. I give You thanks.*

"Come sit on my lap," she said to Ike. "Come sit on my lap the way you used to."

Ike took two or three quick steps backward; Theodore did the same, as if he thought she would be asking him next.

"*I* will!" laughed Edward. "If that's all you're wanting."

Then he tried to, the big fool. The world's biggest cut-up, that was Edward.

"You feeling all right now?"

"In a minute. Still a little giddy, but I'll be myself in a minute."

A chill went through her. She watched as goose bumps spread over her arms. It was on the tip of her tongue to tell them of the great Stomach Serpent living in her insides. She resisted. It seemed silly now.

Lord, they'd haul me off to the asylum and throw away the key.

No need upsetting the boys with talk like that; they'd want to know what it looked like, what was its name, how much it weighed.

Ike stared back at her, picking his nose again. She'd

have to put a stop to that. Dip his finger in red pepper, that might work.

No. No need keeping a boy from being as ugly as being a boy meant he had to be.

She had sucked her thumb as a young'un and on into her first teens, she remembered, when one day her daddy was reroofing the smokehouse and had stuck her thumb into a five-gallon drum of boiling tar. This happened after the man he was working with had seen her standing by and took it in his mind to wonder aloud if she might care to suck on something *he* had the same way she was going at her thumb. He had meant a Mary Jane because that's what he pulled from his pocket, but her daddy had slapped the candy away and yanked her over to where the tar was cooking. She'd thought he was going to dunk her headfirst into the tar and it had been almost a relief when it was just her thumb.

She'd screamed and her mama had come running, scattering a yardful of chickens every which way.

The tar had fried her skin and her mama had tried any manner of unhurtful ways of getting the tar off so she could check the damage underneath.

Ella Mae couldn't remember now whether she'd gone back to thumb-sucking or not.

What's that, Edward?"

He'd been saying something to her which she hadn't heard. Or she guessed he had been, because now he was on his feet in front of her, holding out a sweater he apparently meant for her to slip her arms into. She looked from it to his face, baffled, unable to think why on earth he would imagine she was cold.

He flapped the sweater under her nose as if she was some bull that wouldn't move.

"Time to shake a leg," he said. "Get your head out of the clouds."

She stood up dizzily, raking at the air as if that was a thing one could hold on to. It seemed he had in mind one of his *expeditions* for all of them, since the boys were already in their jackets and waiting.

"Oh, I don't want to," she complained. "I don't want to go anywhere at all, after all the running around I've done today."

"Do you good. What you need is fresh air. Drive in the country, that will put you back in the pink."

"In the country? Well, get me my pocketbook." The sweater snagged on the chair. She winced as she poked her hurt hand gingerly through the sleeve. She was trying to read Edward's face. She couldn't believe he really meant *in the country*. Mostly, Edward's expeditions were to the city dump or through the service alley behind the shopping center, where he might pick up discarded packing crates or root in the paint cans behind Sherwin-Williams for the little they might have left in them. Or they'd drive past the four or five red Salvation Army bins placed around town, and if it looked promising he'd have the boys watch out for a cruising policeman while he crawled inside. They'd picked up she didn't know how many rotted lampshades and falling-apart toasters and beat-up aluminum lawn chairs that way. It wasn't stealing, he told the boys, because what he took was what the Salvation Army wouldn't know what to do with in the first place, and he was only saving them the work. It *was* stealing, *she* told the boys. God was toting up the score and Edward was going to have to answer for it one day.

He was holding open the back door for her and waving one arm to hurry her along, enjoying the way she had to huff and puff simply to get on her shoes. "I'm coming!" she cried, suddenly aware that she was happy. She shoved her pocketbook under one arm, checking to see that the stove was off, and the lights, screwing up her face at the dishes that would be waiting when she got back. "I'm on my way! I know you don't want the house to catch afire. You don't even give a woman time to put on her lipstick. Well, I don't reckon I'm apt to run into anyone that isn't used to fainting whenever they see me. Lock the door."

As she went through, he gave her one of his love swats on the rear. It stung enough to bring tears to her eyes, though she raised no objection. If God could show His love by killing babies it ought not surprise her that a man would do it by raising welts.

"More's yours for the asking," he grinned, his lips puckered up like a monkey's, holding himself in a half squat, his arms lifted like he was out to push a wheelbarrow. "Just aiming to please," he added, goosing her. Edward the card. Her angel, her sweet prince, crazy as a bedbug. Back in his good mood again. That was husbands for you, every bit as bouncy as rubber balls.

"Are we going to the Dairy Queen?" hollered the boys from the truck. "Can we have us anything we want?"

That usually was the arrangement on these expeditions. In exchange for their company while he raided back alleys or Salvation Army bins, he'd treat them to anything under a dollar at Dairy Queen. "Sky's the limit," he'd say, "long as I get back change." She wrestled herself slowly and painfully into the passenger seat, groaning aloud, as much to help out the pain as to keep them from hearing the squeaks and rustles as the truck took her weight. She'd worn out the springs on her side, he claimed, so that the truck now practically dragged the ground.

The truck sat idling with a fast shimmy, Edward getting the engine warmed, a strain on his face as he worked the choke in and out, the cigarette in his lips dancing. It sounded like a mess of chickens squawking under the hood. Pistons needing setting, he'd say, or valves wanting grinding (maybe the spark plugs too)—always something. Something to eat up the money, keep them in the poorhouse. Some job needing doing to take him away from her. That thought hadn't occurred to her before: that the reason Edward was forever poking his head into dark corners, fixing things, was so he wouldn't have to be with her. She studied him, intent on finding proof in his face or (in this instance) the backside of his head, since that was all she could see of him now. Wrenching his shoulders down onto the floorboard to tighten wire around the gas pedal, hawking up spit and wondering where he could put it, maybe deciding to swallow it back down for lack of any other place it could go. He was born country, Edward was. You get him outside and all he could think to do was spit. Hawk it up, and spit, each minute that went by, globs the size of marbles. Squashing it with his shoe like a bug, if it happened he was walking.

And since she was looking for proof of his failed love, his spitting alone was enough to provide it. Did a man who loved you hawk up his spit in public, with you and other people not an arm's length away, often as not not even noticing which way he was shooting it, maybe even hitting your own or another person's foot? *I'll be dogged,* he'd say at such times, *par-done moi my aim.*

Of course, it was only part country, the other part was just plain Tom Fool. Lots of people spit, after all, and that didn't prove love had gone out of them. As far as proving stuff went, everybody knew that proof was as much the devil's tool as was his pitchfork and rake. Proof meant nothing. Look at the Garden of Eden, look at the

Red Sea. Did the Red Sea really divide? There were some, even some in her church, who said no, that it just happened the land was parched after a long drought, and after a thousand years' telling of the tale what the scribe finally wrote down was only what the faithful had turned a drought into. Same for Moses and the burning bush or Jesus feeding ten thousand from a few loaves of bread. What this proved was what everybody knew, that it took no special brains to logically explain away what anybody who was there at the time knew was a fact: that a miracle was a miracle and that's all there was to it. Now, you accepted it on faith or trod the path of evil-doers. Not that miracles did not still happen today. Preacher Eelbone had seen Jesus' face in a shaving mirror while brushing his teeth one morning in 1967. In a motel in Rochester, New York, with a woman he had paid for sleeping in his bed, and that one look had put him on the path of righteousness. A baby in Lima, Peru, had fallen fourteen stories, and survived. Without a bone broken. That was a miracle in her book.

Oh, there were a thousand examples every day. Bette Wiffle, for instance, she might be one. To go from what she was Before to what she was After, from over three hundred pounds to having the time of her life in Antigonish, Nova Scotia. Well that took some doing. And Bette Wiffle, she bet, hadn't done it without the Lord's help.

Dancing the nights away, eating whatever she wanted, being whistled at—she couldn't see that it was vanity to want these things, to have what others took for granted. Not to go shopping for underclothes feeling she was a public disgrace. Not to go blue in the face every time she bent to tie a shoe she couldn't reach without half killing herself. Not to stand sideways at stoves or while scrubbing a dish. Never knowing what she was going to fit into. Not hanging her wash up on the clothesline after dark, when likely as not the rain would get it, all because she couldn't bear to think what remark Eula Joyner would pass on a dress big enough to go around ten stringy Eulas, with some left over. *It's gluttony, gluttony, Ella Mae. Read it in the paper!*

How come? That's what she wanted to know. How come Eula got to be wispy and willowy, someone a flashlight beam would go through, when she had no more mind nor feelings than a grasshopper?

God had made a mistake, that's what it came down to. When He said from on high, *you* shall be fat and *you* shall be thin, He had got their names mixed up. He had got everything else right but that much He had got wrong and now turned a blind eye when she chanced mentioning it in her prayers.

The boys were being too quiet and she looked over her shoulder. Ike had rolled himself up inside a spare tire, while his brother was examining Edward's toolbox. It seemed safe enough, but you couldn't forget about those two for a second.

Edward wriggled up from the floorboard.

"Are we ready now?" she asked, not hiding her impatience.

"You don't want to go nowhere less it's first class, do you?"

Slowpoke, she thought. He was the slowest person alive when going somewhere was on the agenda. "Molasses got nothing on you," she grumbled. He got out and sauntered around to the front with his same handful of wire, and bent briefly out of her sight, maybe wiring down the license plate, which had been close to falling off for weeks. She sat remembering her first date with Edward in a car. He had backed into a ditch, then had run over a mailbox. Finally, when they got going, the en-

gine had caught on fire. They had thrown dirt at the
motor and when the fire was out they had sat on the
running board; he told her about how in Borneo on the
South China Sea he'd seen mosquitoes big enough to
haul away a man, and people two feet tall.

Two feet tall? They must have been Pygmies, then!

*No, they were fully growed. It was the mosquitoes that were
babies.*

It gave her a glow remembering those old times.

"All fixed," Edward said, climbing back into his seat.
"Hold on to your horses."

She said nothing. What glow there was had gone. She
had avoided looking at his boarded-up window, at *her*
window, but her eyes had kept sliding back to it. He
could have smacked me in the face, she was thinking,
and I would have liked that better. He could put up a
sign in the yard saying HERE LIVES FATSO, and it would
hurt me less. He could whip me naked through the
streets and I wouldn't be any madder. The boarded-up
window, the window to what she thought of as their love
room, was an obscenity, plain and simple. Try as she
could, it made no rhyme nor reason.

"Here now, stop that!" he cried. "You're going to run
us into a tree!"

She was grasping his driving arm, shaking him.

"What *is* that?" she demanded. "What have you gone
and done to my pretty window?"

He glanced every which way, pretending total igno-
rance. Pretending *which* window.

"Each time I think of it," she went on (and went on
shaking him), "I see red. Have you been sleeping cold, is
that the reason? I would have put on extra blankets, you
only had to mention it."

"Oh *them* boards," he finally let on. He swerved out
into the street, reversed, and started off. The Joyner dogs
began barking. He started whistling.

It would be a cold day in July before anyone could get anything out of that stump when he wasn't willing.

But he was heading toward the Dairy Queen, which took some of her steam out.

Just once she'd like to step inside Edward's mind and find out what was going on in there. It would be teeming, busy as Einstein's. If there was a thing Edward didn't know, it was because he hadn't yet thought about it. She had seen him read straight through Webster's dictionary, doing it out loud when he got to the Pronouncing Gazetteer, practicing what he said was the way you'd say it if you were Eye-talion or French or a Bloody Englishman. And if it was arithmetic he was doing, like how many calories a normal person burned up eating an apple or a leaf of lettuce or even how many you burned just by opening your mouth to *say* how many, why he could figure such sums quick as a flash and leave your head spinning while he went on speculating why he was normal and she was abnormal since what she ate hung around inside her like iron to bloat her up the size of the Goodyear blimp. And all of it through one mouth, he'd say, it's a miracle your mouth ain't worn out by now!

"Everybody in the mood for a treat get out your money," he said a few minutes later, wheeling into Dairy Queen. The boys let out a shout, crowding up front to see what was there to see. Four of the six parking spaces were filled, a few old grumpy couples but mostly high school boys gathered around the slide-up window. Looking to see what girls they could pick up, Ella Mae guessed—and they would, she had no doubt of that, given what the world was coming to. Some of the boys drifted over a little to get a good look at Edward's truck, poking each other, acting silly-like. They always did that. Edward said the truck was a classic, that was why. "A custom job from the word go," he'd say, and two or three times a week reported what he had been offered for

it. As high as three hundred once but of course Edward
had refused. The truck would be up on blocks in the
back yard the day he died, stripped of its doors, engine,
windshield—anything that torch or chisel could pry off.
He was at the slide-up window now, giving his order to
Estelle, and now and then turned a skinny head her way.
Mercy, she said to herself, those two seem to have a lot to
talk about. Probably checking up on me, she thought,
comparing notes on what I've had from here this week.
What she had was supposed to be a secret between her
and Estelle, but Estelle had a soft spot for Edward and
she would tell him. That woman had been nothing before she and her husband bought the DQ franchise and
now, with a million dollars in her pocket, she thought she
was hot stuff. Too cheap to hire anybody, working separate shifts so they never got to see each other. Some said
Estelle was loose; she couldn't say to her own personal
knowledge, but what any man could see in someone that
skinny was a riddle to her. Hair up like a ball of concrete,
fresh from the beauty parlor, a row of rhinestone combs
from McCrory's dime store sparkling above each ear.
Tawdry, that's what she was. And skimpy on the ice
cream lots more than her husband was. *If you was an alcoholic, I'd have to cut you off!* That's what Estelle would say
to her, which was why Edward was ordering. *I sell it, but I
don't eat it myself, which I guess you can tell from how thin I am!
Good for the business too; if I told you some of the proposals I've
got from back here I'd be arrested.* Fred Joyner swore he had
walked by late one night and seen her on the floor with a
policeman named Cecil Roach. According to Fred, you
could see Cecil's cruiser parked in the back most any
night, and he wasn't the only one.

It beat her how a body could take any joy from sin-
ning. How they could live with themselves, never mind
having to face up to the Lord and retribution.

"Feast your chops on that!" Edward said, climbing in and shoving a banana split into her hands. It bowled her over, his extravagance, and for a second her tongue was tied. Ordinarily he'd only let her have a teensy cone.

"I declare," she finally said, "you must think it's my birthday!"

"Live and let live," he cheerfully replied. "You never know what ill wind tomorrow will bring."

The boys scooted into the back, for once not arguing over who had more and insisting the other be made to switch. Instead, they were asking where they were going, did they have to go home yet. "That's for me to know and you to find out," Edward teased them, though even a dunce could see he was heading the truck out of town. At the traffic light where Ella Mae thought he would turn, he went straight on. Straight on toward the river bridge, toward Gaston Township, toward country. Toward what after all these years she still thought of as home. "Ummm, this is good!" exclaimed Ella Mae, thrusting the dish up under Edward's nose in case he wanted any, but he shook his head and kept his eyes on the road, bent over the wheel as anxious as if he was running the Indy 500, though he was going no more than thirty miles per hour. He hadn't ever been one to have a heavy foot, thank the Lord; whether he was going one mile or five hundred, he kept to the same thirty, usually collecting a string of honking cars behind him, their drivers raising Cain. Only one car was back there now, a couple sitting tight enough together to be glued, probably heading out to the River Drive-In Theater, where *Bloodsuckers* and *Honeymoon of the Vampire* were playing. They hadn't gone themselves since the admission price went up. "Steep, everything so steep," Edward said. "Two steps lost for every one you take."

The couple behind whizzed past, unglued now and

wanting to show off. The boy pitched his arm out the window, throwing up a finger that she knew was meant to be obscene though she pretended she didn't. Riffraff, she thought, you couldn't take to highway or town without seeing them these days. The church had lost hold, the devil turned loose upon the world. Ella Mae hated these people who whipped by so fast they missed all of God's beauty—missed everything. The automobile was an instrument of the devil, her mama had claimed; she would never ride in one and never did either until the day she was hauled in a purring hearse to the cemetery where at last she could rest in peace. Her mother had been old-fashioned, no doubt of that. She wouldn't know what to make of things now.

Ella Mae savored the last bite of banana, the last squirt of syrup, trapping it between jaw and teeth to prolong the taste. She rolled down the window and threw out her plastic dish and paper napkin, ordering the boys to do the same if they were finished: "I don't want you getting chocolate all over your clothes," she said, "nor on any of your daddy's doodads back there, neither." Their trays went whirling in the breeze, Ike's to snag on a bush beside the road while Theodore's did a tap dance on the hard surface. "Get your arm back in," she instructed Ike, slapping at him, "before a car comes along and snatches it off." Her face felt gritty; she got her Avon compact from her purse and examined herself in the tiny blue mirror. Beads of moisture lay above her upper lip—lace of the virgin, her mother had called it. Virgin *Mary*, she had meant, because when Jesus was born Mary hadn't fought and cussed like most women did. She had only pressed back against the hay and, while Jesus came, had given Joseph her tender look, evidencing not the slightest sign of pain save for that line of sweat along her upper lip.

The Avon Lady hadn't been by in some time. Ella

Mae would have a good order ready: more of this pan-
cake makeup and a lipstick and could be a little of that
rose eye color, though Edward vowed he hated it. There
was much she'd like to have, but little that Edward
didn't hate so, she'd just have to wait and see, play her
cards right and see what extra she could get out of him.
The Avon Lady didn't press, that was one thing to be
grateful for. "Oh, I'll just put you down for the small at-
omizer spray," she'd say. "Don't fret about the money,
you can pay me when it comes, I know you're good for
it." The minute she left, Eula Joyner would come flying
over, curiosity to kill the cat and mad as a hornet because Avon, like Fuller Brush and everybody else, knew
better than to call at the Joyner house. Well, she had
better to do than mind Eula Joyner. The tires had a
whump-whump like knots had been tied in them. It set up
a vibration that discomforted her, and she couldn't find
a good spot to rest her hurt finger. She had to keep from
thinking about her finger or she would break into tears.
A flash flood, as Edward would say. Think about anything. She wished there was a radio, but Edward hadn't
yet got around to attaching the aerial or replacing a
tube, whatever was the matter. No, he had time to board
up windows but not to fix the radio so a body could
enjoy a ride. So many new houses going up through here.
It had been called The Flats when she was a child, because of how the river would rise and cover it, but now
there was a dam way upstream, so the area was safe or
supposed to be. The houses, hardly yet a year old, lined
the road like a rank of beat-up dusty hen coops. Run-
down already, which is what happened when you got
trash moving into them. Not a tree left standing. Flowers
set out in lard or coffee cans—tacky, in her view. Ahead
was a mailbox made out of a plow. She noticed Edward
eyeing it too. "Cute," she murmured, and he nodded,
saying he would have painted it orange, not white.

"You and orange," she said, "you'd paint your grave-
stone orange if they let you."

"Nothing wrong with orange."

The boys piped up: "What's orange?"

She told them to *shoosh*. "Shoosh," she said, "we have
heard enough out of you two to last a lifetime." Ike
poked out his bottom lip, a hurt look on his face. Well,
her remark was unfair. Boys had to ask questions, how
else would they ever learn? That was the one advantage
a human had over monkey and polecat: he could ask and
find out what was going on. He could pray, that was another.

She stifled a yawn, glancing over at Edward in the
hope that he hadn't seen. A drive always made her
drowsy. Sometimes, if the boys were minding their P's
and Q's, she'd even fall asleep—denying it, of course,
when they said, "Mama, your mouth was open and you
were snoring to beat the band." "It's all that weight
you've got to carry," they'd say next. Meaning no harm,
but getting her goat all the same. In the paper last week
she'd read of a man weighing 750 pounds. Now that was
fat, that was truly fat, that was a man with problems. At
the circus, she'd seen a woman tip the scales at close to
500, and she had a mustache to boot, poor thing. For a
dollar more, the barker said, she'd take off her clothes
and show all, just step inside the tent. Edward hadn't
budged. "She ain't got your ankles," he said, "and her
teeth ain't nearly the match of yours." She'd banged him
with her purse, knowing he was funning her, for even
Edward could see that woman was twice her size.

"There she is," announced Edward now, meaning
either the river or the bridge. In the old days, what you
clearly meant when you said that was *bridge* because the
river was ugly as could be. The old bridge had floorboards that went *clickity-clack* for the length of three football fields, making you think you'd fall through any min-

ute, and wonder why it was so necessary you got to the other side. It had aluminum girders forty feet high, the whole thing shook, and if a car passed you going the other way, it would take off your paint. The new bridge was nothing, it was the same as being on the regular road, and you couldn't see a lick of water. The way she felt, and Edward agreed, if you were crossing a bridge you ought to know it. As for the river, it was so muddy and thick, someone with paddle feet could walk it. It was that way from its red-dirt bottom, from mill dye, and from all the scum the likes of Eula Joyner chunked into it. Spotted with tiny islands of debris washed up in a twist of vines and snaggletooth foam.

In a minute or two they'd be hitting Gaston School, which was the one she'd gone to as a girl. She and Edward too. They hadn't known each other then, being separated by too many years, though some of their teachers had been the same. All the meaner ones anyhow, teachers so mean they'd as soon slap you as look at you. Though not her, naturally. For the most part, she'd been Miss Goody Two-Shoes, so quiet and backwards they said moss growed on her.

Old times, they seemed to hang around you like a spell of bad weather.

Year after year with nothing changing, time so slow you'd swear it was tied down. And then there was Edward, her sweet precious.

The time Ella Mae first set eyes on Edward he'd been wearing black Navy trousers, brought home along with his mustering-out pay and his brass ashtrays made from cut-off ammunition shells,

and the general fighting experience he didn't like much
to talk about. He had been a pretty sight: fence-post
lean, his white T-shirt that had his Camels rolled up in
the left sleeve, his hair all yellow crew-cut, and his face
shining like he'd that minute stepped out of the washtub.
Maybe he had too, because this was early one morning at
his mama's house when she'd gone there to check on a
job she'd heard about. Something about a woman over
Garysburg way needing a few days' help shelling peas
and willing to pay for it, that's all the job amounted to or
all she could remember of it now. But it had brought her
to him. She had walked out from her place that morning
just after sunrise and waved down the Halifax bus,
which came by twice each day, once coming and once
going, and she'd rode that to the first crossroads out of
Garysburg. Then she'd had to walk four miles through
flat country ugly as any she'd ever seen. She didn't mind
the walking, being accustomed to that. She'd got lost
though, and directions asked for at farmhouse doors and
of sagging old men standing by mules out under trees
hadn't helped her none.

But Edward's mama! His mama had taken one look at
her sweltering out on the porch, with her hair strung
down over her face and not so much as bonnet, hat, or
whisk broom to protect her from the sun, and she'd taken
pity on her.

"Oh gracious me, you poor thing! I couldn't hear you
knocking. I wouldn't have heard brickbats against the
door, not with us going like magpies in my kitchen. Now
don't stand there drooping, child, hold yourself up and
come on in. It ain't much, I admit that, but it's home.
I'm all filled up with help, thank you, but the least I can
do is offer you a nice iced tea!"

Four women, one of them blacker than Moses and
taller than a chimney, were in the kitchen, all but the

black one seated with their knees spread around a five-gallon lard can or stewing pot, and their own lap pans spilling over with peas. Unshelled peas over every inch of floor and more out on the back porch waiting to be brought in. They all said "Hidy" and examined her as if indeed she was a sorry sight, something belonging to a race not their own. But friendly, just the same.

A glass of tea was poured from a white enamel jug that had a rooster's red head painted on it, and this was placed in her hands.

"Now sit right down here and tell us how far you've come and what your name is. I declare, people have been knocking on my door from sunup to sunset all week long, you'd think everybody in the world wanted to shell my peas. I'm putting these up, you see, and then me and Edward, that's my son back from the Navy, we are going to put a table out on the main road and sell them to any sensible person wanting to pay twenty-five cents a jar."

She could tell she'd walked into another and better country because out here they were all smilers and talkers and not once had they gone into whispers over her weight, or let on that they even noticed.

"Peas!" they said, "we got enough peas here to pave highways and feed China both!"

Edward's mama hired her anyway in the end, because another hand or two wouldn't hurt none, she said, and because by that time she could see Edward liked her. He'd come out from a back room slicked up in his tight Navy trousers and the Camels rolled in his sleeve, laughing as he said, "You women make more noise out here than the Japs bombing Pearl Harbor." And he'd gone around the room, shaking hands with these ladies, saying how pleased he was to make their acquaintance, finding a nice remark to pass on this one's dress or that one's hair and letting them know how they were all so young and

pretty he was liable any minute to drop down at their
feet in the worship of them. He was the smoothest man
alive, she thought, as fancy as corn silk. His face lit up
the room more than sunshine through the windows, and
if he was a mite full of himself, if his vanity needed landing gears, she didn't see how anyone could blame him.
When her turn came, he hitched up his hands on his
hips, wiggling his ears, saying for the whole roomful to
hear, "Now this one is a lulu. Wonder what her name
is?" And while they snickered and poked at each other,
he picked up her hand and brushed off the wetness of
peas and came down with his back stiff to plant a hot
tongue kiss square in the middle of her palm.

"Look at Ella Mae," the black woman sang. "She's got
a face like a sunset and goose bumps all over!"

"I do believe," another chimed in, "these two young
folks have gone and fell head over heels in love!"

It was true. Her heart sailed, to look at him, and his
every look back made her fling peas out across the floor,
whooping out her wonder and delight as her hands came
up to hide her red face. All the while the women chortled
and poked good fun, his mama worse than the rest, and
Edward went on bonging his eyes at her, pleased as a
king. Now and then rising up to scoot close up to her, to
hover behind or beside her chair, as if what he meant
was to pour off some of his own blessings on her.

And so that first day with him had gone until, at the
end of it, all his confidence rolled off him, his sauciness
plain up and took flight. So that after he'd walked her
across fields to where her bus would come, he'd had to
kick a thousand cans and leap a thousand fences before
he could work up courage to ask would she be his girl.

"If you want me," she'd said, hoping, as her lips closed
on these words and her own eyes sought the shy relief of
ground, that he would know she was promising more

than that. You can have my whole self, is what she wanted to say. My whole self, and if ever I prove to offer less, the Lord Himself can come and chop my head off.

And she meant it yet. She wouldn't change now what she had chanced then. Even though all the talkativeness had gone out of him and the light had left his eyes, so many years having come between; his truck tires were going *whump-whump* on the road, *whump-whump* the same as her soul, but she wouldn't take any of it back. My whole self, she thought. All I am and would be is his.

The road climbed and swept around and there off to the left was Gaston School. Without her asking, already Edward had his arm out and was slowing down to make his turn.

"Not much, is it?" he said. "But maybe you'd like to show the boys your old homeroom."

She patted his leg, wiped her cheeks dry.

"Yours too," she said. "Don't forget yours."

The schoolhouse seemed smaller now. Not a blade of grass grew in the packed dirt yard and what trees there were had been twisted every way a child could twist them. Edward crawled along, unable to make up his mind where to park, going on by the front where there was plenty of space—just as she would have done in his place. Somehow it didn't seem proper, even now with the yard deserted, to park in the slot which had the principal's name stenciled on a white post. Omar T. Something-or-other, a new one on her.

"Reckon this'll do."

He drew up beside the clapboard building that had been the original school. The boys began shouting to be let out. Theodore squeezed through the window, kicking at her shoulder with his foot to boost himself. Then Ike followed, getting her in the same spot. Black and blue, she thought, I've been black and blue since the day those two were born, brats, nothing but brats that God forgot to finish. Edward got out too. She watched him walk his quick pigeon-toed walk over to the side of the building, and made a bet that he'd hide himself in the bushes there and do his business. He was bad as Fred Joyner, having to use the bathroom the minute he got away from one. She watched his puny hips (but they were adorable, what she'd give to have a behind like his) do a fast wiggle as he shook himself, and caught the flash of his zipper as he turned. He was like an ostrich, one leg behind a bush and he thought he was safe from prying eyes. Not that she would see anything she hadn't seen before. Edward was not exactly modest about what was hung between his legs. *Got over it in the Navy. A man has gone as many miles as I've gone ain't ashamed of showing his pecker.* Of course that was after having a beer or two, when he was feeling his oats. Try to get him out of his underwear when he was going to bed and you'd have as much fun strangling a horse. His trouser pants came down over his shoes, she noticed; she'd have to remember to turn the cuff under or certain people would be talking, saying she had forgotten how or was plain too lazy to sew and look after her man. Too fat, that's what they'd say. *Land-sakes, Ella Mae, how you manage to do as much as you do with all that blubber is a mystery to me. I'd be tuckered out carrying just a third of what you carry.* This morning at the supermarket she'd caught a bunch pointing and shaking their heads, and the check-out girl had the gall to say to her face, "It's hard to keep our Hostess Cakes shelf full with you as a customer, Miz Hopkins."

She slid around and got her feet touching ground, taking time for her body to rearrange itself for the fresh indignity of standing. She waved a get-on-with-you hand at the boys who were hollering "Look at me! Look at me!" like they'd struck oil. All they were doing was swinging on a limb of stunted, droopy pine, Theodore upside down with his shirt over his face, and Ike hanging by one hand like the part-monkey he was.

The brick addition to the rear hadn't been constructed when she'd gone to school here. The part she walked by now on her way to meeting Edward was the lunchroom, and on down was the new gymnasium. Children of her time had to bring their lunch in a bag when they had it to bring. A cold potato sometimes and maybe a molasses biscuit and maybe an apple that had been wrapped in paper and stored in a barrel under dirt for winter-keeping, though it would be soft or dried-up anyhow. There was the new football field stretching away in front of her, coming to a halt at the wire fence which a row of flat identical box houses backed up against. One of the goalposts was down. She could make out where they'd tried to draw lines with lime through cantankerous crab grass. There hadn't been any organized sport to enjoy in her day. You'd form a big circle and throw a ball at the group inside, and that was it. Those outside had always aimed first at her, out of the sensible proposition that the easy ones should be eliminated early. They'd got her always with the first throw.

Yah yah yah, Blimpo's out!

A basketball backboard had been nailed up here. Hanging from the ring, itself no more than the hoop from a barrel, was a tatty net that looked rotten. Edward was standing under the basket, his hand full of pebbles, trying to throw them in. He said it was harder with rocks than with a basketball.

"I don't like this school," Ella Mae said. "I never did."

"That so?"

"They taught a person how to read and write and reminded us how we were supposed to behave and after that it just stopped."

"God knows what I did here," Edward said, "because I sure don't remember."

Elsewhere in the yard was an iron climber contraption for the younger kids, and six swings, and over there a tire hanging from a rope between two posts. All the swings had bird mess on the seats. There was a seesaw also, and a fortress thing made out of logs.

"It's easy to see children only go to school these days so they can play," she told Edward, who nodded absentmindedly, no doubt thinking his own deep thoughts.

It was an ugly, forlorn-looking place, like a factory making parts for something that wasn't used anymore, like Henry Ford's Model-T.

"Takes you back a spell, don't it?" Edward spoke so soft and pleasant, as if so much in communion with her own spirit, that she had an urge to turn and fling her arms around him.

"Look at how tiny those seats are!" she gushed, her nose pressing at a window now. "You reckon I could fit in one of them today?" Her voice came out too loud, sounding trashy even to her. The fit had always been a tight one, and there were jokes every year over whether she could or couldn't. One year they had made her sit on a bench by the wrap closet. She wished the boys would stop their hooting and hollering. Probably they weren't even supposed to be here. The busybodies in the tract houses by the fence were likely watching, probably thinking they had come to break in. She tried to remember what it had been like, what she had felt, the day she first walked into this school. But it was mostly blank, she could recall little that was specific, had only the general sense of herself as an unweaned orphan-child making first entry into a more civilized, more fanciful and elaborate world. In the books she'd read here, about visiting Uncle's farm and all that, the children didn't get strapped, the father didn't drink—everyone was happy just doing what they did.

They had said prayers. There had been the anthem to sing. There was homework to hand in if you had any, though that would come later, at a more advanced grade. There were pictures to cut out, pictures to crayon in, stories the teacher read you out of a book. Many, like herself, had never seen a real book before, outside of the Bible. That's why she and Edward had their *Reader's Digest* condensations and a nearly complete *World Book* encyclopedia set out in plain sight—so Ike and Theodore wouldn't grow up thinking home was a queer place to find books. Sometimes on TV she'd see a room in a home filled with nothing *but* books, and she would make sure to point that out to the boys.

Miss Grimes had been her first-grade teacher. They had made clocks and pasted on numbers and hands with flour-and-water glue. Miss Grimes would move the hands and you'd have to stand up and make a stab at what time it was. She remembered thinking it strange that Miss Grimes spent so much time on clocks. Their parents might or might not own clocks, but it was the sun they told time by. Where the sun was was what mattered. She recalled that the teacher had made a sun cutout, and pasted that above blue paper water, and she had told them this was the Atlantic Ocean. The Atlantic Ocean was bigger than the farms they came from, bigger than all their farms lumped together, bigger than their

farms and a thousand cities. *One day some of you will dip
your own two feet in it, maybe even sail upon it.* The whole class
had laughed. *Yeah,* someone had said, *me and Buck Rogers.*
Later on, it had been that cardboard sea with its yellow
sun that she pictured when she heard grownups whis-
pering about all the ships the U-boats sent down. It
struck like a snake, the U-boat did. It was a sinister, silent, unfair thing. Only the Nazis had them and that was
why teachers told you to remind your parents to pull
your green shades down.

What a scruffy lot they'd been. Not scrubbed clean the
way her children were before they went off in the morning. The boys' hair slicked down with Wildroot Cream-
Oil or table grease, cut from the ears in a line so straight
you could see the size of the bowl their mamas used. A
sea of big ears, big hands, and feet big from going bare-
foot so much. Eyes that, even when dull, gave off a rabid
quality, the kind of cunning alertness or rancor of an animal in a cage. Clothes mostly worn-out hand-me-downs;
new or old, all came from a mail-order book.

The boys were on the swings now, calling to be
pushed. Black as crows from rolling in the dirt, and every
bit as noisy. Edward went over, saying he'd push them
right into the next county, he'd make them think their
stomachs were coming right up through their throats.

"Not so high," she warned him, "you don't want them
losing their supper."

"Look at me!" Ike was crying a minute later. "I can
touch the clouds!"

"Push me! *Me, me, me!*" cried Theodore.

She had never been one for heights herself. Swinging
made her giddy, even a porch swing sometimes, and af-
terwards she'd walk around half-dazed, thinking her legs
had disappeared down through her shoes. The earth all
rubbery the way it was if she smoked one of his cancer

weeds. Edward appeared to be enjoying himself. He was a good father, there wasn't a better father in the whole world. And so good-looking. His face was scorched dark from working in the sun, though he had these white lines around his mouth from that frowning habit of his. Muscles rippled in his white arms, that were slender as any woman's. She had more hair on her own, she reckoned, than he had on his. He had no backside to speak of, that was the miracle. No, his behind was flat as an ironing board. He didn't have much chest. His shoulders went straight out and they were bony, which some people wouldn't like, though she liked it just fine. "If you were perfect," she used to tell him, "what would I have to complain about?" His Adam's apple was maybe too prominent, not that she minded. One of the most endearing sights she knew of was seeing Edward coming out of the bath to put on a fresh shirt. The way he had of buttoning the collar button first, then stretching his neck way up out of the shirt, his chin uplifted while he turned his head this way and that. A chicken hatching, that's what it put her in mind of. She laughed every time.

What's touching your funny bone? he'd ask.

Oh, nothing!

Exactly like a baby chick, even down to his eyes, which had that funny way of rolling around loose in his head. Then he'd stick a leg into his trousers and go stumbling around exactly the way a hatching chicken would. "Don't ridicule the master," he'd say to stop her laughing—and of course she'd laugh all the more, because he would go on stumbling, never learning which pants leg was which. You'd think with feet small as his he wouldn't have that trouble or that the Navy would have taken it out of him. He'd told her a thousand times how so many nights the ship's alert would wake them from their slumber and they'd have to quick throw on their ducks or beegees or whatever a work uniform was called in that man's Navy, and rush up on deck to shoot a cannon out over the water at nothing he said he ever saw. He said the brass would once in a while let the hands sharpen up on birds flying by, or on treetops if there was an island handy. His feet, though, they really were tiny. He could walk around in her high heels lots easier than she could.

"Back in a jiffy," he said now. And she saw him strolling off in the direction of a Dempster-Dumpster he had spotted, the boys tagging along. She didn't know—but wished she did—what was going on in Edward's mind with this visit to the school. Being around schools made him uneasy, she knew that. It hurt him that she had more education than he, and that soon the boys would too. Although you'd never guess it by listening to him talk—he was smart, smart as a whip—the truth was that Edward had dropped out of school in his fifth year. Partly, so she understood, because he was fed up with it, and partly because his daddy had got sick and someone had to help his mama out. He was apt now to be touchy on the subject. Edward would be mortified if he knew she had discovered his secret, the secret being that not long ago he had enrolled in the LaSalle high school correspondence course. With his brains and hard work, he'd probably have his high school equivalency degree pretty soon, depending on how much time he could find to put in on it. The ad she'd seen in her *Photoplay* said the La-Salle degree was recognized around the world; one of the people who had taken it said the degree was good as gold, and a real step up in his life since he got it. She always knew when Edward was doing another lesson because he'd come in from the garage with his sheepish, half-holy look and stand around waiting for her to say something—anything—to him. She'd say, "What you been doing in the garage, honey? Is the truck broke down again?" and he'd put on his cat-swallowed-the-canary smile, saying to her "Don't be *flippant!*" or "What an *exotic* day this was!" or "I *abhor* the *fallible* mind, don't you?" Or he might offhandedly mention that Peru produces 55 percent of the world's supply of vanadium, the largest refrigeration plant in the world is in Argentina, also the largest grain elevator in the southern hemisphere. And did she know that Canada has eight rivers more than 1,000 miles long? "Name them, I bet you can't." Or he'd say, "I bet you a dollar to a doughnut you don't know the square root of . . ." whatever it was. Oh, he was full of himself once he got going. Most times, however, if you happened to mention the advantages of a good education, he'd blow a gasket. He would quickly put in that not having one hadn't hurt him any. You couldn't deny this, either, since it was Edward who ran the freight yard. He ran rings around that Mr. Hargroves, not that he ever got any credit for it. But let him stay out sick one day and you wouldn't get a minute's relief, the front office calling every five minutes to find out where this or that was, who had shipped what to where and when, for God's sake this and for God's sake that, trying to make Edward think he'd made a mess of things.

It beat her how he put up with it.

They were coming back now, the boys slung to either side of him like roped calves. They wore their hound-dog look and were whining, which meant that Edward had decided they'd best be going. "Shuffle off to Buffalo," he'd say. He was carrying over his shoulder a bicycle tube and lumber scraps and under his arm was a blond desk top and what looked like a bunch of loose-leaf notebooks. His pockets were jammed full too. One time, she remembered, he had come home with eighteen wigs, and hadn't been content till she'd tried on every one.

"Time to hit the road," he called, "elsewise the dark will catch us before we get to your daddy's old home-place."

She whooped with delight. Edward was being sweet to her as pie and she could hardly believe it; it had been a month of Sundays since he'd been willing to take her out to the old family house. She fell in behind him. She wished, though, that he'd stop calling it her daddy's place. It was her mama who had kept it up, kept it alive. Her mama who had seen to it that the animals were fed, that hogs got butchered, that ham and bacon got smoked. Her who made lye soap, cooked and saw to the house, propped up fences and one way or another saw that the seeds got in. No, her daddy spent his time rest-ing in the shade, down at Cal's store punching for prizes on the illegal punch-board, or worse. *I'm going up Beef Road,* he'd tell Mama, *You and the Queen of Hearts stay home and worm the dogs.* Beef Road was where the squatter gyp-sies lived; if a man found nothing there to his liking, he went on to Providence Line, which the law couldn't close on account of some curiosity in its geography.

The day already had lost much of its light. She wished Edward would speed up, but knew how he'd take that suggestion. According to him, more killers were on the highway than were in the pen. They were out in their flashy cars going lickety-split and putting anybody who got in their way in the hospital or cemetery. And the po-lice were in on it. Otherwise, wouldn't the jails be full? And Detroit was in on it, and OPEC, and all the con-struction companies that built these super-duper high-ways in the first place. It would be much better if all we had was dirt roads like in the old days. Driving fast was like any habit that you got addicted to, it changed your whole way of seeing things, your whole way of being. Your blood pumped faster, your nerves were on end; not just the highway, but everything else sped up too. All systems were Go, and going fast. That meant everybody and his brother. Everything that wasn't tied down was being stole, not just TV sets but wives and sweethearts too, and most of all, man's pride and dignity. Homes falling apart, crime in the street, half the world on strike and the other half on welfare, kids with zip and pep only for whatever would speed them up the fastest, and how could you blame them when that was the only example set for them?

That was the kind of lecture he might give, and however right he was, she was in no mood for it. Her blood was racing, she couldn't wait to see the old homeplace, and she didn't want to chance Edward telling her to whoa-up. Already she was hungry again. Some peanuts would be good to chew on. Her mouth felt a little dried out. A soda pop would hit the spot as well. But Edward would hit the roof, so she might as well keep quiet about it. Actually, it wasn't so much hunger as it was needing something for her hands to do. Her poor finger. Grit your teeth, old gal, and put up with it. Folks have put up with worse. She'd seen scalding water thrown on a moaning dog. Esther Glover had walked around since day one with a growth on her cheek big as an egg. Another woman she knew had spent six days down a snake-infested well; Ruth, last name she couldn't pull out of the hat just now, had been beaten black and blue and then gone out and sat in a locked car until she froze to death, rather than go back in and be beat up anymore by her gob of a husband. On her own street, a girl had been raped and hit with a tire iron not four feet from her front door. All of these people, and hundreds of others she could think of, were far worse off than she was. A hurt finger could put a steady ache behind your eyes, it could make you believe you were going blind. But a hurt finger was a trifling matter and did not bear thinking about.

Houses and fields passed by. Shilow Church was not far ahead, set back in a willow grove. She watched for the steeple, pointing it out to Edward when at last it hove into view. The services for her mother had been held at Shilow Church. A sunny day, not much different from this one. The men, a dozen or so, had mostly huddled in the yard, keeping to small groups so they could shield each other as they did their drinking. Her mama had wanted to be buried in the cemetery next to the church; her daddy hadn't allowed it, saying the Shilow graveyard was too run down. Pure orneriness. What a shame. You couldn't even be buried where you wanted. You didn't have nothing and never had nothing and then you didn't have that.

"Smoke in your eyes?" asked Edward.

She had pulled a tissue from her purse, had it crumpled up against her face. *Blubbering,* she thought, *that's all I'm good for.*

"I was remembering Mama and the day she died," Eila Mae said.

"Thought so," he nodded.

Edward shook his head as if death was incomprehensible to him. The boys piped up, their voices shrill, wanting to know who had died, what were they talking about? *Death,* she was of a mind to say, *and one day it will claim you, too. Now you think time stands still, but one day you'll look back and marvel that it was over so fast.*

The truck had slowed even more, Edward letting it coast down a long incline, turning off the motor to save on gas. At the bottom of the hill, as so often happened, he couldn't get the engine started again, and had to pull off onto the gravel shoulder. He said nothing, nor did they. She and the boys had sat so often in ditches or on gravel that they had grown resigned to it. He got out and raised the hood, pulling a rag from his behind pocket. There was so much about this man that continued to amaze her after all these years. The rag, for instance, that was always in his pocket, usually hanging there, even when he was dressed up. Even if the truck didn't break down, he'd come up with one reason or another for stopping. Every five miles or so he had to get out, check the tires, check the oil. If she bothered to complain, he'd mention a man he had known once who had had to junk his brand-new car all because he never thought to check the oil.

"Here's the trouble," she heard him say. And of course he had to come around to her window and show the filthy, smelly thing to her. The potato. Plain old Irish potato. About a year ago he had rigged up a potato on the fuel line to stop a leak. Every third or fourth day since then, he'd gone at her potato sack, got out another one, and put it on. He could have gone down to Acme Auto Parts and for a dollar got exactly what he needed, but no, he had to have her potatoes. He grunted, squirming back under the hood, and when he stood up again, she studied him closely to see if he'd made a mess of his clothes.

He winked. She smiled, shaking her head at the mystery that was Edward.

An orange cast bathed the rim of the next hill. She gasped when she saw it, clutching at Edward's driving arm. "The woods," she said, "the woods are on fire!"

He had his head stuck out the window, already peering at it. They crested the hill, and suddenly the full sight was thrust upon them, shocking in its magnificence: a huge, orange ball of sun, only the sun more awesome than any ever seen. It vibrated with heat and everything in its path was glowing. Edward's face and clothes were

bright orange, the truck hood was bright orange, everything inside the truck was lit that wonderful orange. One
of the boys behind her was violently twisting her hair,
squealing with rapture, quite unaware of what he was
doing. She moaned in ecstasy. She tried to shout *Look!*
Look! Look! But her mouth was dry, she could make no
sound at all. Edward's eyes were shining, his mouth
hanging open, a hand thrown up to shield his eyes. The
sun's center was blinding. Ike was jabbering, jabber-jab-
ber, she wished he'd hush up. Edward was driving faster
now, as if what he wanted most was to deliver them
directly into that awesome firmament. She didn't feel or
hear the tire thumps any longer. It seemed to her that
the truck had found wings, that they were soaring well
above the land.

"If that don't beat all!" whispered Edward. "Godamighty, if that don't take the cake!"

"It's beautiful!" she cried. "If I was a heathen and saw
that, I would fall down on my knees." She would. She
would kiss the ground, go on kissing it, for the earth was
red with Jesus' blood. It kept getting bigger, bigger, heat
rays boiling up from every surface touched, the very air
pulsing. It's so close, she thought, a person could reach
out and touch this sun.

They tumbled down a small hill and momentarily lost
its mighty center, then they topped the hill and there it
was again, bigger and nearer. The color seemed more
crimson, changing with each second. It seemed to be sitting there, waiting just ahead in the road's middle, droning at them. Edward's hand locked on her knee, squeezing. Squeezing and unsqueezing, hurting her, though it
did not occur to her to ask him to stop. The sun seemed
to rise up. It swole, and hove, and rolled nearer. "Godamighty," he whispered. "Great Godamighty!" Finally he
let her knee alone, but only so he could use that hand to

pound on the steering wheel, to bang on whatever he could. He was dancing in his seat, twisty as a snake. "It's right here!" he said in a hush. "We're riding right into her!" The road dipped and the sun dipped with them.

Then a thing happened so curious and so unexpected she could not at first believe her eyes and ears. Edward's face was pressed inches from the windshield; he kept snapping his head right and left, whipping it back and forth so fast she was afraid he would screw the whole thing off. He beat on the steering wheel with both hands. His face went knotty, his leg shot out as if he meant to kick it through the floorboards, and all this time he was making these sounds like Flipper on TV. Like nothing she knew as Edward.

"Edward!" she shrieked, "what's wrong?"—and took to steering with her own hand to keep them on the road.

He shook his head fiercely, throwing off her hand, throwing it off wrathfully each time she put hers back. The truck zigzagged down the road, throwing up dust, kicking up stones. Quail fluttered out from a bush and in one breath were gone. The sky was red. It was red and empty but for that groaning sun, and them.

Edward was crying, that's what it was: he was crying. *As I live and breathe,* she thought, *has the world come to an end?* Edward never cried, he was her rock and foundation and she could hardly credit what she saw. The tears rushed up, catching in his throat, spittle on his chin now, and he went on making that terrible sound, throwing up his shoulder to hide what he could from them. Ashamed, his mind not his own, yet still throwing off her hand. He had lost control. He was sobbing desperately now, sucking in air, trying to speak. Saying her name. Slapping at the boys as they wrestled over the seat to get a closer look at him, slapping blindly, as if hornets might have been after him. Blubbering like a baby as she sought to steer

the truck back over the yellow line, to steer sense into
him. A Cadillac car came honking and streamed on past
them, a tiny Virgin Mary mounted on the dash while a
hula girl shook in the rear. Her eyes had time to take in
that, time to catch red treetops swishing by. She had
time to holler at him, "Edward, don't wreck us. Get hold
of yourself!" Part of her was glad: she was glad the shoe
was on the other foot, that it was Edward acting like a
mad dog and not her. He did speak at last, a tangle of
throaty words making no sense to anyone. Something
about how he had tried, how he had hoped against hope,
how it was all up to him now. "You, Ella Mae, I'm taking matters in my own hands, doing what I got to do!"
Nonsense words, no rhyme or reason to them, and much
of it not words at all, just sounds, the ache of what they
cost him. In church she had seen people like this, people
in the grip of God's power and trying to shake it off, to
deny God's love, speaking gibberish in that instant before their spirit submitted and flesh became radiant and
the Word became God's. But never Edward. Edward
said these people were fools, that inside of a week they'd
be drinking and whoring again, that their tongue-speak-
ing had nothing to do with God, it was only hatred of
their own ugly insides, their own ugly lives, doing it to
them. That or stupidity, he'd say. But he was wrong. The
tongue had finally been laid on him.
    "God *lives!*" she suddenly cried. "Doesn't He live? Isn't
He wonderful! Aren't you thrilled!"
    He smacked at her. He did. Before her words were half
out, he lifted his fist and swung it straight at her face. His
hand caught her cheek, burning, bringing tears. She
shrunk away with ringing head, horrified and speechless,
shocked by the snarling rage that showed in his face.
Venom, nothing but venom! The tires thumped crazily,
swerving over dirt, rattling the truck. It flashed through

her mind that the truck would explode, that Edward
wouldn't be satisfied until he had them killed. Hatred, so
much hatred in him! She could see in her mind the truck
jumping the ditch, smashing into a tree, every one of
them ripped open and bleeding, dying. She saw herself
going toward her grave with the mark of his hand on her
face, and it was this that helped to bring her back. She
wrenched at the wheel, shoved his foot from the gas. *I
will not have this*, she thought. *I will not. I will not depart my
life with his mark on me.*

Ike was bawling, Theodore up at her ear shouting,
"What's wrong. Why's he acting crazy. Why'd he hit
you?"

"It's all right," she shouted back. "You boys calm
yourself, in a minute everything will be peaches and
cream!"

With this the tension went out of Edward. His face
broke out in a flash of what amounted to a shameful
grin; he straightened up, bobbing his head and wiping
his pocket rag over his eyes, those eyes softening as they
regarded her. He could still smile. He still could. Peaches
and cream, she had said, and that seemed to be what he
was looking for. The truck slowed. They were barely in a
crawl now. "It's for your own good," she heard him say.
"That's all I meant to say." His voice strange, straining
to be voice at all. "I been a good husband. It ain't my
fault what's happened to you. I know you don't like it
either. I'm only doing what I have to. I don't mean you
no harm." Amazed, she studied him.

Through all of this, the huge sun hovered before them,
rim gracing the earth, land and trees on every side blaz-
ing.

Ella Mae had no notion at all what this man was talking about. She was in the dark. Nor would she let herself
think about it, now that his madness and temper seemed

over. But she was hurt and bewildered all the same, biting her lips to stop their trembling. To stop herself from arguing back at him. "Nothing's happened to me, Edward," she murmured. She patted his sleeve, tentatively at first, then with more assurance. "Not a thing is wrong. Me and the whole family is as happy and content with you as kittens. Take it easy now. Stop and compose yourself and you will be fine in a minute."

Her voice and her stroking were calming to him. She could see that. He nodded, drying his nose, offering what she took to be a contrite smile. Yet she could see more. She could see he hadn't said all he wanted to. That he couldn't, now. Repentance and suffering, sorrow and doubt, seemed to surround him. He looked to her like a little boy would look, one who knew he soon was to do something he shouldn't, something terrible and mean, and now wanted her assurance that she would go on loving him whatever the deed.

Then the look was gone. He patted her hand back, threw off his somber mood, saying: "You're a fine woman, Ella Mae. There's lots you have put up with."

The sun tilted. They glanced up, gasping, for it seemed to be rolling down on them.

"Look out!" she cried. "Look out! Oh, what is happening to us?"

The road swept down. They took it and, quick as a heartbeat, the fiery sun was gone. It had disappeared. It had not gone down, nor did tree or hill obscure it; it simply was there one second and then gone. Immediately, the sky darkened. A chilling wind stole up out of nowhere, bending the tops of trees. Swept past, and then it too was gone. The sky rippled and darkened more. A purple strip churned up from the horizon, curdled and spread. Then that deepened and black night was suddenly upon them.

Ella Mae sat rigid in her seat, watching all this. She wanted to take back these latest minutes in her life, to let it start over from the second they left the school yard. To drive into the sunset, to marvel at it, and praise God. To have Edward stay Edward and not go all vicious and ugly. To have him kiss her hand, declare his eternal love. She shivered, closing her eyes. Such a flood of foreboding I have now, she thought. Nothing but bad news coming my way. I can feel it coming and I know there is nothing I can do to stop it. *Oh, help me,* she thought. *Show me the way.*

But she had to open her eyes and wonder about that: she didn't know whether her appeal was aimed at Edward or at God. Didn't know who to aim it at. We ought to head back, she thought. Lock and bolt the doors, hide away in bed. The sap has gone out of me. If I was a drinker, I'd drink; if a smoker, I'd smoke. Lose myself in sin, if sinner is what I was.

But she wasn't a sinner. She wasn't a dog, to lie down and quit. *So gird your loins, old gal,* she told herself. *Gird your loins and stand up to all the devil can throw.*

She shook Edward's sleeve. "It's got so late," she said. "I'm not even sure I could find my old homeplace in this dark."

"Oh, you can find it," he said. "You could get there with your eyes closed, I expect." He was collecting himself now, coming back to his true self. Lighting up a cigarette. "Ought to be getting close now."

"I don't know," she said, letting her weariness drain out. "It's all changed on me."

That it had. They hadn't gone past hardly a spot she could say she recognized. She pinned her eyes to the side window. Looking for the pine grove which hid the nice spring water, for Aunt Ruth's big house with the roof tower, for the Beef Road turnoff to Aunt Blanche's place,

for the windmill that a farmer had put in a field, made
out of a Flying Tiger airplane with the teeth still painted
on. Looking for the creek where a boy named Henry
Adams had hit her with a rock. Looking for Cal's Store
and the Goody's headache powder sign. Looking for
Spook House, where a man had killed his wife with a
hatchet, then kicked over a chair to hang himself and let
his only child come in to find him. Looking for any trace
of the eighty acres her mama and poppa had owned.

But it was all new and different. Hairpin turns were
gone from the highway, the dips had been flattened out.
You saw fewer fences, fewer houses, the old barns were
gone. You could go miles without glimpsing a lightning
rod. Livestock roamed free in wide fields. Today there
would be crops she couldn't even name. Houses were of
brick, boasting fancy lawns and gates. Family names
swung from black wrought-iron posts and not one yet
was a name she'd grown up with. It was different even
down to the color of the earth. In her day, tree had been
on a par with cleared ground; you could look at it and
know that God had a stake in what went on. Now it was
all man-made, and man seemed intent on raking it clean.
Raking it flat. Raking all the spirit from it.

She thought all this, and felt herself getting madder by
the minute. "Hold it!" she cried, flinging her words
out—"Stop this thing! It ain't here. My homeplace ain't
out here. It ain't nowhere around here!" Rebuking herself, rebuking Edward, and the dark. Furious that nothing could be counted on. That everything changed.

But Edward drove on. He blew out his smoke and
squinted up his eyes; he smacked the dash to keep the
panel lights going, and drove on.

All right, she thought, don't listen to me. Nobody
does. Keep on going until we all drop into a hole.

More flat fields passed by. You hadn't been allowed to

1 3 7

plant tobacco here in her day. You had only three money crops then: cotton, corn, and peanuts. You might get a little bonus from soybeans. A few dollars on top of that if you went to the trouble of hitching up a wagon and trekking fresh crops to town. Saturdays, that would be, following a fly-swishing mule's tail into town. Selling your tomatoes and okra, your sweet potatoes and Idahoes. Cabbage and butter beans. Your table corn. Your cantaloupes and watermelons when finally they ripened. Maybe a few pounds of grapes off the scuppernong vine, a bucket or two of winesaps. You could take in your eggs, if you had any left over. Your collards and turnip greens. Cucumbers. Your rutabagas, carrots, or squash. Then the long ride home. Another day, you'd say at day's end, where's the dollar?

That was the summer run. In winter, when the belt rubbed backbone, you might again make that journey to town. In the open space between White's Motors and a shoe store too dusty and empty even to have a name, you could throw up a rope between two trees, hang out clothes already worn down to their threads, and sell these for a nickel or dime to people worse-off than you were yourself. Another day, you'd say at day's end, where's the dollar?

She'd gone from that to getting hit by the man she loved. Without warning. Without even thinking, just lashing out. Shouting in a crazy voice that whatever he did was for her own good. Accusing her. Threatening her, stirring her mind with visions of the doom that was waiting up ahead. This was not Edward. Other women told her how they got beat black and blue. They went on radio and TV to tell of it. Some crossed her own street to tell her. *Not Edward,* she'd say. *Not my Edward.* What could she tell them now? Lie? The next thing would be stealing, and then drinking after that, and then denying

Jesus. One slip and there you went, that's all the devil needed. And it seemed to her that she'd already slipped; without knowing it, she had, and that's why Edward had hit her in the first place. *It's for your own good,* he'd said. He always said that, it was his explanation for everything he did. If he wrapped his cold feet around her at night, that was for her own good, and if he left his whiskers in the sink or his socks on the floor, that was for her own good. Boarded-up windows, that too, she reckoned, would be for her own good. Her daddy had been the same, whipping her with hickory sticks that he said hurt him more than her, whipping Mama when she intervened, whipping dogs and claiming that too was for their own and the general good. *It's not my fault,* Edward had said, *what's happened to you.* Ugly. She'd never seen anyone so ugly as then. Yet what had happened, where was her sin? *I'm only doing what I have to,* that's what he said. What did it mean? How could he look at her like a fist was knotted up in his brain? Hatred pouring off him.

She swung around, her hand up to open the door. Thinking she would jump out if she had to. "Stop the truck," she shouted. "I mean stop it now! Turn around. I've gone far as I'm going!"

It was no use anyhow. Nothing was. She might as well give up. Her homeplace wasn't on this road. It wasn't anywhere up here. It had been wiped off the map and the map changed, another map brought in that had Ella Mae Hopkins and her mama and daddy's scab-face acres nowhere on it.

"Go home," she ordered. "Take me back to where I know I am."

The truck rumbled on, Edward blowing out a cloud of smoke like that was what he had to get through first.

"It's the truth," he said. "I don't know where your old turnoff has got to. It does seem to have disappeared."

I don't want to hear any more of your truths, she

thought to tell him. I've had all of you tonight I can stand. But she kept her mouth clamped shut. Speaking would do no good. Nothing would. She was plain burned up. She was quivering with rage, with the senselessness of things. That Edward would turn on her, yes, but that she couldn't even get back to the place where she was born. That was the last straw. That her place and her mama's place could up and disappear, that it was as much buried as that Indian Mound. Buried and gone.

They passed a road sign: EUSTACIA, forty miles straight ahead. There was a creek-crossing too. Then a string of old Burma-Shave signs, some fallen down. She could see her life the same way she saw them—ELLA MAE BORN . . . ELLA MAE WED . . . ELLA MAE DYING . . . ELLA MAE DEAD . . . BURMA-SHAVE!

Edward slowed down. He got the truck backed up against some stumps, and turned around. "We could keep looking," he said. "You're the one always hankering for your joy rides."

She let that pass. She wanted to spit at him.

"Swamp," he said. "Swamp and briar fields, that's all this next stretch is."

She turned her head, looking back, when they again went by the EUSTACIA sign. It was a puzzle why, but she had never come this far up the road. She'd always gone the other way—to Gaston School, to Shilow Church, to town. She wondered if her life would have been different if she had taken this direction. She wouldn't have Edward; she wouldn't have Ike and Theodore. Money and good times might have been waiting for her; she might have been thin.

Some of her rage was leaving her. Her insides rumbled. She hungered for something to lick on. Something without taste or smell, which you could eat and eat and always have it there.

"No sugar in that fingernail," she heard him say.

She dropped her hand back into her lap. Picky-picky, she thought, it's picky-picky every breath I take. I can't do nothing right.

"Boys gone to sleep?"

She stretched her neck and saw they had.

"Pretty dark now. Hardly see your hand in front of your face."

"No, and wouldn't want to," she snapped.

But she took it back. He was trying to be nice now. Trying to show he was not all Jekyll-and-Hyde. The truck seemed to run easier, heading back. She could hear Theodore snoring. Gritting his teeth the same as she had done. Cold air blew up from the floorboards. She shivered. Out past the throw of Edward's headlights, the world shook like a weary ghostland.

It wasn't Edward's fault that she weighed a ton. No more than it was her doctor's, or all that starch, or supermarket sweets, or Dairy Queen. Dr. Spratt said nothing about glands, he said it was nerves. "You eat because of your nerves. And your nerves are shot because of how you eat. It's a chicken-and-egg question which comes first. Not much I can do, short of locking you up or wiring your mouth shut. Did that to a patient once and she gained sixty pounds."

Spratt didn't know doodly-squat about *fat*. No more than he knew about chickens and eggs. God created the first chicken and the chicken by herself took care of the egg. He created the chicken so we would *have* eggs, as every fool knew. If she went to the trouble of telling him some days she ate no more than fifteen hundred calories, his mouth would drop, his eyelids too. Then he'd cackle, much as calling her a liar to her face. He wouldn't believe it made no difference what or how much she ate. Spratt was like everybody else, he thought it was greed, vile evil greed, and went on cackling, saying if she wanted to go on killing herself, that was up to her. Some doctor. Ten dollars a visit, wedged in between squalling children and beer-belly grumps, and nothing to chew on while she waited. Knowing Spratt would ask what had gone into her system. Even Edward was better about understanding than Spratt. Edward *tried* to help. Like his trick of going through her purse to find food she might have hid. A rotten dog. Last week he'd pulled out a slice of apple pie. What a scene! Mrs. Ibena Gates from next door had been passing the time with them in the back yard. She'd all but rolled off her cinder block, laughing. And Edward laughing too, taking a bite, saying *It's fresh, I'll say that for it!* Naturally, Ibena Gates had run right across the street to tell Eula and Fred. They'd all stood out in the Joyners' ugly yard, cutting up, repeating what she had told Ibena: that the pie wasn't for her, that she'd wrapped it up in wax paper and put it in her purse, meaning to take it to Old Lady Wrenn down the street— too sick and crazy to cook for herself and not a soul caring whether she lived or died.

Which was the truth. Old Lady Wrenn had pus in one eye and wouldn't talk to you, but if you brought her a dish, she'd mew like a cat and turn you every which way, looking for more.

They were approaching Gaston Hill and the turnoff leading down to River Road. She strained her neck, looking to see if she could make out from here the outdoor movie screen. She couldn't. But a memory tumbled in on her. Down that road, on or about her eighth year, an old man, half-monkey and unable to speak a single word other than *monkey*—had been discovered living in a cave near the river, within walking distance from her own home. He had been there for years, unbeknownst to any living soul. That's where she would like to be. In that hermit's cave with a big rock pulled in after her. I'd stay there forever, she thought. And all of these people whose love I can't depend on could forget Ella Mae Hopkins. They could go on their merry way. They'd never again have to pain their eyes looking at me.

Half an hour later, it wasn't home he drove up to. No, not a word about his intentions, about her desires; it was Edward the Serpent driving big as you please up to the hospital emergency door, saying *"Git out!"* in a voice she wouldn't have used on spoiled child or dog.

"Out!" he yelped. "Git out!"

She sat bolt upright in her seat, wrenching her head uncomprehendingly from him to the hospital door, where a man was crouched with his face pressed to the glass, squishing up his nose to get a good look at her.

"Have you gone plain loco, Edward? I got no business here."

The man with the flat nose must have thought she was saying something to him, because he backed up with a doubtful shake of his head. Only it wasn't a man, she saw now, but a ghost-faced boy in a wheelchair, teeth and ears too big for his face. The boy gave a last malevolent glare at her, stuck out his tongue, then wheeled himself out of sight.

"I mean what I say," Edward went on. "I've put up with that swole finger long as I'm going to. I'm taking matters in my own hands. You head straight in there and tell the first doctor you see that I said to fix up that finger."

It was his do-what-I-say-or-else voice. She had heard

him use it on her no more than a dozen times in her life. He reached past her, opening her door. She pulled it shut again. Her mouth was twitching and she couldn't stop it. The boy came back in his wheelchair, and he'd brought another person with him, his mama, who had wispy hair, the same protruding teeth, wore a mustard-green polka-dot dress, and carried a baby in her arms. A nurse passed behind them, yawning.

It seemed peaceful enough in there. If Edward had done it differently, if he had come around and nicely opened her door, if he had said *I'm with you, honey, all the way,* why, then she might have been willing. She'd have chanced it. But she wasn't budging now. He could kill her, she told him, but she wasn't moving.

Edward had both hands against her shoulders, white-faced, grunting as he pushed. "Git out!" he barked. "You are behaving like a child, a stubborn child who ought to have his neck wrung. Like talking to a stump." He brought his foot up. She flinched, thinking he meant to kick her; instead, he brought his dirty shoe against her hip, shoving—but he could only rock her.

"Stop it, Edward!"

But he went on grunting and straining, white with rage.

She was moaning now, hiding her face from the crowd assembling behind the hospital door. Each time she peeked out, the wheelchair boy was dragging up another gawker. Edward had never before humiliated her like this in public. She would not have thought him capable.

"Please, Edward!"

"If that finger falls off," he said between breaths, "don't blame me. Don't say I didn't do my dead-level best to make you see reason!"

His heel ground into her side. There was a lump in her throat and she no longer cared who was watching, no

longer cared for her own life. Her marriage was over; she
would never again be able to look into his eyes, to feel
pride in him. He had ruined everything and she'd just as
soon die.

Gradually, she and Edward both became aware of
someone's presence beside the truck. It was a useless presence, she felt, meaning neither harm nor good, and if her
eyes acknowledged that it wore a uniform, that it had a
face one could call human, she was not touched by the
knowledge. Edward had delivered them both over into
the devil's hand. The devil's work was under way. That
was what Edward wanted. His hatred and contempt of
her was so great that he was willing to walk hell's road
himself just to see that she got to her destination.

"Move on," the voice said thickly. She saw a face bent
low at Edward's window, blacker than the night behind
him. "This here zone is an emergency zone. You got to
move on."

She laughed. She didn't know why, but she did.

"This here zone is for emergency vehicles only," the
thick voice continued. "Maybe you can't read. Maybe
you can't see any of them signs posted every ten feet."

She looked for the signs. They were there but it was
dark and she couldn't read them. The waiting room behind the emergency entrance seemed brighter now. One
of its fluorescent tubes was flickering. Everyone had gone
from the door now except the wheelchair boy. He was
puffing on a cigarette and squinting from the smoke just
as Edward did. He had a long thin arm and the fairest
skin and it seemed to her he was smiling at her. It was a
beatific smile. The hand holding the cigarette, well, it
was holding it all fluttery-like, the way a girl would. He
smoked and squinted and then the smile came her way
again. It seemed to be saying to her, Ella Mae, I offer
hope. I offer beauty, is what I offer. Thou shalt not de-

spair. The wheelchair boy was in the Lord's buffer zone; he had been sent down to observe the proceedings, to offer what hope he could, and to report back on what inroads the devil's work had made.

He was an angel. She turned, meaning to express her amazement to Edward in those very words, but her heart sank back down the second she spotted Edward's ugliness.

"I can read all right," he was telling the dark creature outside his window. "I got me an unwilling patient, that's my trouble."

The face again dipped down to the window, peering across at her. "She looks frisky, but I never known friskiness to kill. What's the lady's emergency?"

"Show the officer your finger, Ella Mae," Edward said.

She wanted to get it out while she was still able, to say to them, Can't you two stop your ignorant chatter long enough to behold the Lord's angel sitting pretty as you please over there in a wheelchair? But Edward was opening his door and climbing out. He was telling the officer that her arm was swole up like a fire hydrant, that she'd been nothing but a bag of nerves from it for weeks on end, making everybody's life miserable—but would she do anything for herself? No, she just went on mindless as a doorknob.

Her angel had opened the hospital door a few inches in order to hear all this. She half-expected him to raise a hand in her defense, to say at a minimum, *I am on that woman's side!* He sneered, and the orange tip of his cigarette cut an arc through the darkness.

Edward and the uniformed man went through the door without speaking to the wheelchair boy, and disappeared inside.

Then the boy suddenly got up out of the wheelchair,

crossed the room, came back with a magazine, sat back down in the chair, and began flipping the pages.

A few minutes later Edward came out. He had a doctor with him, and they stood at the door the longest time, talking, now and then gesturing out toward the truck. Finally, the doctor slipped several objects, too small for her to identify, into Edward's hand. Edward got out his wallet. Each time he passed another dollar to the doctor, he would first lick his fingers. The devil's money. Caught on the edge of night, both looked like they had come up out of separate holes to have these secret dealings. Then the doctor tapped a finger repeatedly on Edward's chest before disappearing inside.

The wheelchair boy looked asleep. He had been visited by God's spirit in angel form without even knowing it. God had given him the use of his limbs to walk across the room and pick up a magazine, he had done so, and now he was a cripple again, sleeping, and none the wiser. Eelbone would have to be consulted on this matter: God moves in mysterious ways His wonders to perform. What the human eye perceives is more than a little passing strange. It is not given to us to know His master plan. Which one of us can say why you are the size you are, why it is Eula Joyner was made to wear cowboy boots and not you yourself, why it is left to the likes of Bette Wiffle to enjoy the good life away yonder in Antigonish, Nova Scotia, and not you yourself? When my limbs were locked with those of loose women in a thousand motley motel rooms up and down the length of this land, who would have said that too was part of His master plan? When I sought after rotgut day after day and slept nights sprawled out in doorways on city streets, who would have predicted God in His own way was preparing me for His ministry? All we can say for sure is this—if God makes cripples walk and blind people see; if He can turn our lives around and change king into pauper, pauper into king, we ought not to be surprised. It is His will and we can no more not bend to it than the leaves on the tree not bend to wind. A dead stump, given water, will sprout green twigs, and green twigs, thriving on richest fertilizer, can just as quickly perish. The same with you, the same with me. Do you think there will be fat people in heaven? Or will we all be Olympic athletes passing through the Pearly Gates? If we haven't bodies like those we have now, what will we have? They tell me today scientists can take out human brains and put them in pans of water and that these brains are alive as you and me. Eyes can go into sockets where other eyes were, limbs can be sewed back on, hearts borrowed and livers swapped for new. Take Adam and call him Exhibit A, and Eve and call her Exhibit B. Adam has a sex-change operation and becomes Eve. What is sauce for the gander is sauce for the goose, and Eve has an operation too. Is it God monkeying with us or is it the surgeon with his scalpel? Some would say the latter, but I would remind you the shiny purse can not be made from the sow's ear, that the surgeon winds up only with what was there all along. Cain may wear Abel's eyes and limbs and vital organs, including the evil heart, as comfortably as he can wear Abel's suit of clothes. The time has come when you can't tell the two apart. No more than a hair's breadth separates Exhibit A from Exhibit B. You might find the fact disgusting. You might say to yourself, Well, those two are hardly worth looking at, I'd as soon accept that as climb a tree and eat coconuts. But closed eyes no more change what's in front of them than the absent ear changes the sound the tree makes falling in the peopleless forest. Human beings have put a lot of pressure on God. We may not like it, *He* may not like it, but earth is no longer a pretty place. It was not meant to be, or there would have been no need for heaven. It is *ugly, ugly,* Ella Mae! And I grant you, you are not pretty to look at. You are definitely one of God's ugly people. It would not be in the category of progress, however, to give your liver to Fred Joyner, your legs and arms to Eula, to give what was left over to your dear Edward. Jesus at Calvary did not say to one, You take that pain, and to another, You take that bit. He said, No, sinners, I shall take it all. And then he said, "Eli, Eli, lamah zavachtani?"—Why have you forsaken me, God?—to show he was human like the rest of us.

Oh, how that Eelbone could talk! Your ears would be smoking before he was done, but when he was done, you often felt worse off than you did at the start. How come I'm so blue, he'd leave you thinking, when I've just been shot full of the holy spirit?

"Here's home!"

She jumped, the sound was that startling. Thinking the sound was inside her mind and not beside her, thinking it was her angel in the wheelchair gone inside to announce to her that they had arrived at God's kingdom, don't steal the silverware. It was Edward, though, and this was her own yard he'd pulled into. He was stretching, yawning, saying it was going to be good to hit the hay. The boys came up groggily, complaining.

"Be Goddamned!" one of them cried. Ike it was, slapping at Theodore, who apparently had stepped on his foot. She did not move to smack his face. Nor did she raise her voice. It came to her that she could not move at all, that she did not want to move. That she could not bear to leave the truck and go inside this house she hated now. She could see the window—see what had been a window—without turning her head, the boards darker than the rest of the house, gloomy as Satan, more permanent somehow. Like a disease about to spread, or one that had already spread, though you couldn't see it. A shiver went through her as she thought this. A sense of abiding dread. What had been plaguing her all day, the foreboding that had been tracking her footprints all week, had manifested itself. It was in there waiting. She had only to walk through the door and it would claim her.

"You going to take all day?"

Now Edward would come around to her side. He would choose *now* to open her door and stand there bowing like a fool, inviting her to step down. She shook her head, fighting to hold back her tears, hiding her face. Where his hand touched, skin turned numb, her heart lurched; it could not have been worse had Edward been a hired killer sent to lure her forth and kick in her brains, what rhyme or reason she had left.

"Git out, baby!" he whined.

Her head snapped up. *Baby, indeed!* Now it was *baby*, baby this and baby that, when all the time he had his knife twisting at her insides. He looked stupid to her, stupid despite his menacing and cavalier air; he and everything around her looked stupid and doomed, with not a touch of anything that could ever be redeemed or even was worth redemption. Let it all rot, she thought, all of it! Let it rot and let us rot, then we can be done with it. Let us be dung upon the ground. Now that her heart had been broken she could see life for what it was, and her own part in that life for what it was, and Edward's part—and the boys too, don't forget them. They were all dung upon the ground. God's dung, maybe, but dung nevertheless. The Divine Hand had written as much. It had written it in Ezekiel 1:2 when it prophesied that the slain of the Lord would extend from one end of the earth to the other, to one end and back again, that the earth would be covered with the Lord's slain, that

they would go unmourned and unburied, that while they
might walk upright for a time, they were for that time
and for all time dung upon the ground. Not *like* dung,
but actual dung, whether breathing or unbreathing,
whether living or dead. Dung, nothing but dung. No, not
Ezekiel but Jeremiah, Chapter 25. There it was, proof
from the Divine Hand, if proof is what was needed when
it was staring you in the face the whole time. Which
must be what Eelbone meant when he spoke of how the
earth abideth forever. Dung abideth, that's what he
meant—dung and rot and filth, whether it was this
house or this yard or Edward bent at her window ap-
pealing to her with whiny Adam's-apple voice and his
mean snake eyes: "Aw, come on, Ella Mae, you don't
want to set out here and freeze!"

That's exactly what she wanted to do, to be sitting
here through this scrunched-up night so in the morning
every busybody and his brother could troop by, laughing
as they declared, "There sits what we thought of as fat
old Ella Mae the Sow, now turned into what she was all
along, a fat lump of frozen dung."

"Stubborn!" cried Edward. "I never seen the like!
Worse than any child or mule!" His fist banged on
metal, he stomped on the ground. "What's got into
you?" Your meanness, she thought to tell him. Your
meanness that overflowed and which I tried to sop up
before it spread, but which spread anyhow until all I can
see now is dung. She was crying, little sniffles that
burned her nostrils, grief that pressed like a hot iron
against her whole face. "You go on in," she whispered.
"Go on. I aim to sit here for a while."

"You sure?" He backed up, tripping over some un-
evenness in the ground and flailing his arms to upright
himself. "You not going to do nothing crazy, I hope."

She wiped a hand under her wet nose, studying him,

marveling anew why it was that the crazy ones always thought it was the rest of the world gone cockeyed. His look at her was strange too—not Edward's look but the look of a person whose path had crossed hers by accident and couldn't quite make up his mind what it was he saw. Only that he didn't like it. Cold, she thought, so cold he could put hatchet or bullet through me this minute, turn his back on me and never think of me again. She wanted to reach out and grab him by the ears, shake that look away. But she couldn't move. Her lips were dry, her tongue swollen up inside her mouth. She couldn't speak. All she could do was dredge up a whimper from deep down, think to herself *Edward, you've not been nice to me. Edward where has your love gone?* To sit there in the truck the law said was as much hers as his, shaking her head at the mystery that was life, thinking *Edward Edward Edward,* yet unable now to hitch up a single word to that stranger's name.

"All right then," he said, drawing close, spitting his nastiness out, "if you going to act that way I can too. Anytime you want to be this contrary, I can beat you by a country mile!"

The truck door closed on her like a gunshot. It was how the door had to be closed if it was to stay closed. All the same she took it as yet another insult, as Edward's way of saying *Woman, this is the last straw. Woman, I give up on you.* He really was turning his back on her. He was saying *Stew in your troubles, Fat Woman, you don't mean beans to me. You can sit out here and think your black thoughts till hell freezes over and when it does I will come out here and sweep the dung away.* She watched him prance away over the grass, taking strides that lifted him up out of his shoes. Full of himself now, she thought. Now that he had caught a hint of what getting shut of her was like. Shoving the boys on in front, those two who all this while had stood rooted by the back-door steps, struck dumb, gawking at her with their big eyes. Theodore stuck out his tongue at her, making some nasty sound. Edward swatted at both, driving them inside, then followed himself, closing the door. That was what he wanted, to close the door forever on her. To be single, footloose, and free to chase Winnameer Riser or high school girls, to fall down dead drunk in alleys or on motel beds anytime he took the notion to. That was the man thing to do, it was what men sold their souls to have. Now he could have it. He could go out and lay down on the floor with Estelle at Dairy Queen, or with a rat if he wanted to, for as of today, as of this minute and hour, he had cut himself loose of her. He wouldn't any longer have to go around town with a fat wife around his neck like a hangman's noose.

The kitchen light came on. She saw Edward's face appear at the sink window, his eyes shielded as he peered out. "Go on looking!" she said aloud, trying to put into her voice the same kind of whining ugliness he would have in his. "You can look out that window till you're blue in the face but you won't see nothing! You could ask me. I've looked out that window a thousand times and I know all you can see is night looking back! If you had to go and put boards on a window, you could have put them on that one where Eula Joyner's always sticking her nose!" She scrunched up her face, taking back those words. She wasn't talking to him, what talking there was to be done some lawyer with the gift of gab could do tomorrow. He wasn't no husband of hers, he had proved that today. She remembered the tale of how Jesus, seated by a well in Samaria one day, had a woman come up to him with her empty pails and he said to her, *Woman, go and call thy husband,* but the woman, thinking Jesus some no-account bossy fool, answered back, *I have no husband.* And how Jesus, smart as a whip, next said to that woman, *Thou hast well said I have no husband, for he whom thou now hast is not thy husband.*

The same here, she thought. That man yonder at the window can go wrap himself around a barber pole, for he is no husband of mine.

Edward's face withdrew. The boys' faces immediately replaced his, tinted yellow as though they had jaundice, hands around their eyes like binoculars. *A little child shall lead them,* that's the thought that floated into her head. But lead *who?* Lead *where?* And which one, if God had to choose between Ike and Theodore, would He choose? Ike was neater on the whole, but then he was older. Theodore, on the other hand, was lots quicker between the ears. He'd taken to potty training with the snap of a finger, for instance, whereas Ike had gone on year after year not much better in his habits than that scrawny parrot Eula used to keep in a rabbit cage full of dead sticks on top of her bureau. A smile came to her, remembering that affair. One night Edward had snuck across the street and hunched down under the Joyners' window to speak in a squawk exactly like the parrot's. *Eula is a cracker! Eula is a cracker!* he'd called over and over before finally scooting away. And those mindless Joyners never had caught on. Not a bit. The next morning at the crack of dawn, they'd both come running over proud as peacocks, bringing the mangy bird with them, saying, *This here parrot talks. You ought to heard it last night cutting up a blue streak! What'd I tell you, we going to make us some money out of this bird yet!* And Edward let them go on thinking so, he didn't let on a thing.

She kept on laughing, not able to stop it now that it had started. "Oh, Lord," she said, "those two do take the cake." Because they'd gone on for weeks after that, trying to get that bird to talk some more. Had gone on, that is, until finally Fred—or maybe it was Eula—had lost his temper and killed that bird with one swing of his liquor bottle.

Oh what fools! If a child had to lead that pair, whether God chose Ike or Theodore or the poor unfortunate cripple whose picture was on the March of Dimes poster on her upstairs wall, whoever it was chosen would have to get up bright and early and eat his Wheaties and get off to a fast start or they'd never get nowhere. They'd have to bring lots of filthy whiskey along and call a rest now and then so Eula could glue in her stamps and rub the bunions her cowboy boots made. They'd have to give her all the time she needed to tell everybody how she was flooded under with *bills bills bills*.

There will be no bills in heaven, Eula Joyner—that's what a good leader would say. *Now you just pick yourself up, and carry on.*

Ike's face was gone. Now only Theodore was there, clouding up the glass with his heavy breathing. Probably sitting up in the sink so his legs wouldn't get tired. So he wouldn't have to strain himself. For certain, Edward wouldn't make him climb down. No, the fact that cleanliness was next to godliness wouldn't occur to them. They'd as soon sit in a plate as eat off it. They'd clean their toenails with her knives and forks if she let them or if it ever struck their minds that toenails were part and parcel of God's glory and required a good cleaning now and then. They'd wallow like pigs, if not for her.

"Well, they can go ahead and wallow," she murmured, "because I'm done with being dragged through the mud for them."

Still, Theodore looked cute. He looked harmless and helpless and just *cute* with his face plastered against the glass. Like his face was this very minute being chiseled out of perfect air. She loved his complexion. His hair was lighter than Ike's or theirs, lighter than corn silk, especially when he was a baby. Especially when it was clean. More than likely it would be him God would choose. Theodore liked leading, seemed born to it. He had the backbone. He'd sooner stand a week in the corner than break down and do a thing you told him. He was plenty good-looking enough to lead, if ever he stopped his mouth from hanging open. She and Edward had spent a lot of time wondering where he had got his beauty. *From my travels,* Edward said, as if that explained anything. *I've seen nations. I've lived side by side with fair-haired people. Maybe when I planted his seed all the time I was on you, I had in the back of my mind some Scandinavian. One of them butter-sucking Swedish gals. Maybe that's how he got it.*

Eula Joyner—to show where God forgot to leave brains—didn't seem to care for her boys. She'd lift a hand to cover her eyes every time she saw them coming. If they threw a can in her yard, she'd be slamming doors and running, as if another can or a ton of them in that yard would be noticed. Oh, she knew what views Eula Joyner held. Old Lady Wrenn, mewing like a kitten, had passed the word on. Old Lady Wrenn reported that Eula Joyner said that too many children put the blight on a neighborhood and there was two she could name ought to be tied to a rail and choked till they were ran over. As for looks, Eula to her face had called them stocky. On the stocky side. Like young white-face steers, she had said.

Now *there* was one to talk, with her hair like a glue pot, with her face like a washed-out road. The nasty piece. She'd be over at her house now, saying to Fred *Wonder why Ella Mae won't git out of the truck? Wonder if she plans on spending the night out there? Wonder if she still have the piles, the hives, the nosebleed and menstrual cramps? Wonder how many pounds she's put on this past hour?* Saying this and other claptrap while standing in her tatty underwear, peeking through her blinds with whiskey glass in hand, yakking the news back to Fred until he loses his mind and throws more lit firewood at her to shut her mouth.

Theodore was tapping on the kitchen window with his knuckles, whether laughing or crying she couldn't say. Whether begging her to come in or telling her he hoped she never did. Then there was a flurry of activity and once more all three were there, their curiosity-killed-the-cat heads lined up side by side, looking every bit like witless ghouls, like some foul-breeding Holy Trinity come with a manufacturer's guarantee to break her heart. If she had had a rock, she would have thrown it at them, broken the sink window and all behind it.

But there was no need, for two of them were gone already, leaving only Theodore still there to dirty up her sink with his shoes. She groaned, pushing her rancor down, concentrating hard to hold it there where her Stomach Serpent could get at it and be content for a while. It exhausted her, this lump of ugliness that kept shoving around inside her. She longed to go in as a loving mama who could stroke her hands through that child's hair. To say to him, putting as much sternness into it as she could: "You best haul your little bottom off to bed now. It's late and you know you got school tomorrow. You know your mama loves you and your daddy loves you and you going to have a good sweet life if you stick with your ABC's."

Edward came to the back door, stared out a minute either at the truck or at her in the truck, then shook his legs and passed back inside. He wouldn't say *bottom*. What he would say was *ass*. Assuming it ever crossed his mind that growing boys needed sleep. *Child, you best haul ass and I don't mean maybe. Ass* was a word Edward liked saying, one more bad habit brought back with him from the Navy and one he'd practice day in and day out if she let him. *Them clod bossmen down at the yard don't know their ass*

from a hole in the ground. All men like that word, it being a
riddle to her. Her own daddy, to mention one. Every
time she turned around or got into the least bit of trouble, *ass* was the word her daddy found: *You can give your
heart to God for your ass is mine.* Reaching for his belt, not
even bothering most times to say it was for her own good.
Or when he was having a knock-down, drag-out fight
with her mama and Mama would ask *Where you going?*
he'd storm out the door shouting *Going to lick ass, where
you think I'm going! Going to git me some!* She hadn't known
then, thinking *ass* was nothing more or less than a short-
ened-up mule. Thankfully, Edward didn't take it that
far. He didn't mean it for women, it was no more than a
word he liked the sound of on his tongue, like *shithook* or
yellow belly or the way, whenever he was mad and after
she had said something mean, like *You're cracked* or *You got
marbles for brains,* he'd rear up on his hind legs without
missing a beat and snap out something like *So's your fairy
godmother* or *It takes one to know one.* Just words, just whatever he was used to finding on his tongue, the same way
Jack Coombs couldn't break himself of the habit of talking every chance he got of the economic *maelstrom* do-
good politicians had got us into and the *socialist hordes* we
had to watch out for. *Well, it's another maelstrom today,* he'd
say. *The socialist hordes were hard at work last night while you
were in bed catching your shut-eye.* Innocent turns of the
tongue, no harm meant, intended only to wake us up—
not like *ass,* which put her insides in a knot and quivering every time she heard it.

Well, he was *ass* now, Edward was. That was all he
was, ass through and through.

He could kiss her ass, that's what he could do, him and
the whole kit and caboodle—for boarding up her window, for taking her on a long drive that went nowhere
except to get her face slapped, for trying to dump her off

at a hospital where some hog doctor could saw off her finger, and now for leaving her alone out here in the cold truck with nothing but her black thoughts for company.

Yes, he could kiss it, he surely could.

"You can bite it," she said aloud. "You can just bite my ass!"

She quickly looked up at the sky out of shy willful stubbornness, fully expecting clouds to part, the earth to roll. Fully expecting lightning bolts. But the sky hung peaceful as you could expect it to with half its ozone gone. Gone in no little part because Eula Joyner had to spray-can her falling-out hair a thousand times a day. Had to chase around with her buzz bombs for any mosquito that showed, though in the meanwhile flies swarmed around her thick as—well, thick as flies.

Hush now, she told herself, don't go dragging the misfits down. Don't heap scorn on one who never had the advantages you had.

Her mouth tasted vile and sorry enough already from using that word. Spit out the bad taste, she told herself. Hawk up your ugliness, retch the nastiness out of yourself. She bent forward, spitting, trying to take it all out. Intending to flush out her system the way Edward would his radiator. *Throw in the Power Flush,* he'd say. *Throw in the Friction Proofing. Drop in a can of Joe's knock-proof STP. Make this old buggy brand-spanking new and sound as a dollar.*

Globs of spit landed on one leg and began sliding down like stomped-on worms. Naturally, she didn't have a tissue. Naturally, you never had what you needed when you needed it. Story of my life, she thought, lifting her dress, sniffing, wiping her mouth and nose. Straining to stretch cloth down to her filth. Ruin this old drip-dry, she thought, what do I care? What have I got to live for now?

She couldn't reach it. Each time she bent forward, her

stomach rolled up under her arms to bounce her back. She leaned against the seat, hassling for breath. Giving up. She let her eyes clamp shut, hating herself. Even a polecat kept itself clean. Even a plain house cat licked its paws clean, and although a rat had lice, you'd have to scratch his coat to find them. She was worse than polecat or rat; her mama would cry to see her like this. She'd holler too. *Did I raise you to walk around with your own spit hanging off you? Is this the thanks I get for working finger to bone sunrise to sunset? Am I never to have no rest from you?* She whimpered, hearing Mama storm and rail at her. Hearing Mama break off a switch, tensing muscle and flesh and screwing her eyes tighter against that second when the switch would come stinging down. Crying in her heart now the same as she had cried it then: *Mama Mama Mama, don't smack me! Mama, I couldn't help myself! Mama, I'll be good!*

She sobbed aloud, throwing up her hands to protect herself, repeating, "Mama Mama, I've told you I'll be good!" Crying like a baby, heaving up her tears and hearing herself shriek the same as she had then. The switch whipping through air, snapping and stinging down—only remembered, but hurting nonetheless and maybe more for not being real.

"Hit me, Mama!" she cried. "I know I am getting only what I deserve!" And in her mind and to her flesh, Mama's springy switch came whipping down.

With wet eyes, she had stared so long through shiny windshield that black shine was all she saw, and then a star came out of nowhere and suddenly swooped down. She let out a gasp, her face lighting up, though the star burned out even as it came to her that star was what it was. Before she could remind herself she ought to make a wish or think what that wish might be, it burned out, leaving the sky blacker than it had been before. Like a zipper in black velvet that had closed, her own shooting star had come and gone in the blink of two wet eyes. Only seconds old yet over too soon for memory to throw it back again across either sky or mind. Gone, with only the feeling to linger on. Like childbirth, she reasoned, when you have forgotten the pain.

But what did it mean, this star? For clearly it meant something. God did not play around in His firmament for the sake of teasing talks. He meant to get news of some kind through to her—yes, He did. He had sent first his sunset, then seen they were not worthy, and taken it back. He had sent this star and then let it burn out before wish could be made, maybe because she was not a fit vessel for wish to be satisfied, maybe because she could think only of herself and not, for instance, of her wedding vows or her boys, who any decent mother would by this hour have sound asleep in bed. Vanity of vanities. What would He send next? And why must He make such a mystery out of it? Why didn't He come right up to the truck and whisper His guidance into her ear?

There I go again, she thought, questioning His every mood. Edward's right, I ought to be roped and tied. I ought to be shut up in a deep hole and made to gnaw on bones for my own good.

She struggled, squirming and grunting, from the truck. Might as well, she thought, I'm whipped anyhow. I was whipped from the start. Between God and Edward I never stood a chance.

Her shoes felt wooden and thin on the ground as she hobbled on in.

The kitchen was deserted. It amazed her, the second she entered, how bright and shiny—and empty—her kitchen was. The table had been wiped clean, neither hide nor hair of crumb or dirty dish could be seen. The sink had been wiped dry, her J Cloth draped over the faucet neat as could be. The mop had been got out and pushed over the linoleum, leaving nary a streak nor a drop of tramped-on food. Her toaster was shiny. They'd wiped the spatter off her stove knobs and the little oven window her mama would have given an eyetooth for. They'd somehow got the dust and grime off the plastic fruit in the bowl now set in the middle of the table. She knew the task that must have been, because the bananas especially had a kind of fuzz cover, put there by the heat and the general filthiness of things. She stood back, admiring how the fruit looked in that new spot. She agreed with them, it looked so much better there than it did up on the counter where she'd kept it—though to be fair she'd only kept it there so Eula Joyner could poke her head in and yodel *I sure wish I had me some fruit like that!*

The five Red Rooster tins holding her flour and meal and sugar, her rice and dried-up potato flakes were put up on the shelf. Every cabinet door and drawer was pushed shut. The table chairs were tilted up on their front legs like you might see in the best restaurant when they'd closed for the night.

It was pretty as heaven, that's what it was. The whole room couldn't have looked smarter had she done it herself.

A note in Theodore's up-and-down hand was stuck with Scotch tape to the refrigerator door:

dear mama we tidy the kitchen for you

She sank down, overcome with joy, thinking *My three angels!* It hurt to recall how only a few minutes ago she'd been calling them witless ghouls, and more.

They'd even thought to spray a dose of Alpine Mist through the air.

She walked on through, saying under her breath, I can't believe my eyes! None of Edward's clothes hung from doorknobs. The boys hadn't scattered theirs in piles all over the house. All the boys' toys had been picked up. All Edward's tools had been put out of sight.

Wonder of wonders, that's what it was.

She felt the way the Pilgrims must have felt, walking into a land of milk and honey. They deserved medals, every one of them. They deserved to have a whole army come up and kiss their feet. If Eula Joyner said another word about children being rubbish, she could just wave this pretty house under her nose and tell her *That's what rubbish done!* Eula's eyes would pop out and roll on the floor.

Oh, she was so tickled she could sing!

On the stair railing dangled another note: *we gone to bed,* signed *The Boys,* and halfway up was a third note reading *hope you feeling more spunky now,* again signed *The Boys.*

Her two angels, her two Aces in the Hole!

But there was nothing from Edward. No sign of his love, discounting what elbow grease he'd used on the kitchen. She came back down the stairs, made a circle of the living room and hall and even went and opened the front door, searching—but no, there was nothing from Edward. In the living room again, drawn back there by instinct, by nothing so much as the puzzle on her brow, it struck her this time that something was missing. Something as it ought not to be. As clear to her as the missing front tooth in Fred Joyner's mouth. She stood for some moments speculating on the vacant space against the far wall, at wheel marks on the floor. The box, that's what it was! The TV set had up and been moved.

"Now why has he done that?" she asked. "Is he putting in more nuts and bolts, or taking them out?"

She passed on out of the room, feeling miffed and put out that he'd moved the box without asking, though for that matter TV meant nothing to her. Except for "As the World Turns" and "Days of Our Lives" and "Family Court" and a few other good shows, he could pitch it into the river for all TV meant to her. Not that she was a regular viewer of these shows, not like Eula Joyner who would put her feet up and waste away the whole afternoon; it was just that it was helpful knowing what went on in the world—so many schemers and womanizers and backstabbers you couldn't believe your eyes. Hardly a single Christian in the whole pack.

Once more she made the very same round, this time collecting the boys' notes, folding them carefully away into her dress pocket. Patting them flat, reminding herself to store them in her keepsake box first chance. She'd keep these cute love notes for all eternity, the same way she'd kept locks of hair from their first haircuts or the twisty dried-up-looking cords that had tied them to her the day they were born, which Edward said was sickening. *It don't mean nothing,* he'd say. *Even a cow or monkey has them. Even a roach does, I expect.* Up there in that box she had their lost teeth, little rocks and soft-drink tops they'd brought in; she had tiny blue socks so small you'd think they'd never seen a foot; she had their report cards from every school year, most of them saying *This child needs to try harder* or *No improvement this term,* and one, in Ike's case, that said *Failed!*—all underlined in red like the teacher had gone half crazy putting it there—*Failed, Does not Pass into Next Grade!* Edward liked to say she'd keep the wax from their ears if he let her, that she doted on them worse than a mother hen.

Her angels. The women they married one day would appreciate rummaging through these treasures. Edward called it silly, but a woman would understand.

She was back in the kitchen now, meaning only to turn off the lights. Turn them off, lock the door to ward off rapists and thieves, then head upstairs and face the music. Face Edward, get on her knees and face God. She didn't think she'd ever have to eat another bite long as she lived, not with the boys being so sweet, not with Edward and the boys working overtime to please her. Though it wouldn't hurt—now that she was here—to open the refrigerator and check that they'd put everything away properly. You couldn't leave such matters to men, men being unable ever to comprehend that a bowl had to be covered, that good home cooking would end up tasting like onion or cucumber if you didn't wrap it right.

"Just as I thought," she murmured, stooping, the cold air swooshing out.

Maybe she would have a teensy bit, maybe a single forkful, that little bit couldn't hurt. It would do her good, in fact. If she tried going to sleep on an empty stomach, she'd only toss and turn, she wouldn't sleep a wink.

"No," she said, "I'll just help myself to a mouthful of this cabbage. There are few things better on this earth than good cold cabbage, when it's been simmered in ham, with a teaspoon of vinegar sprinkled over the top the way I do it."

Ummm, yes it sure was good.

Fred Joyner said an army could march on its stomach

one whole week from a single bite of her cooking, it was that good.

A minute or two later, mad at herself, she shoved the bowl back; then she reconsidered and took it out. There wasn't no use in letting the bowl take up space when there was so little left in it. She took the bowl to the sink, washed it and dried it, and put it up in the cabinet. There wasn't no need in leaving evidence about to fuel Edward's pettiness and bickering. There wasn't no need to put a wrinkle in their nice cleaning-up job, either.

It came to her, hanging up the dish towel to dry, that she was still hungry.

One more little bite, she thought, to keep my rosebush blooming.

On the refrigerator's top shelf, put up front where her eyes must have been closed to miss it, was a giant tub of Dairy Queen ice cream, what Estelle called her come-and-get-it size. Chocolate, the best kind, and going a little runny the way she liked it, with the baby spoon they gave you already stuck in. Poked through the handle was a sheet of pink paper she recognized as one of Edward's yard shipment forms. On the back with Theodore's crayon, he'd written A LATE NIGHT SNACK TO PUT SPARKLE IN YOUR EYES OF OLD LOVE, EDWARD.

He's precious, she thought, sitting down to the ice cream. He's the most precious hunk of man on earth and if ever I breathe another word against him I hope I will be strung up and hung and shot dead as a doornail or a rabies dog.

Near the bottom, her spoon raked against something. It slid off, crinkly and shiny. She dug at whatever it was, feeling plain disgusted, thinking *Those people ought to be sued. This is worse than getting a dead fly in a new Coke bottle.* She reached in with her fingers and pulled up plastic that kept on opening up until it was a full-size

transparent bag like the kind she'd wrap her vegetable
scraps in.

"Will you look at that!" she said.

Inside was a folded-up note on another of Edward's
yard forms. SURPRISE SURPRISE! it said, I HAD ME A BET
WITH THE BOYS YOU WOULD GET DOWN THIS FAR. I HOPE
YOU FEEL GOOD.

She couldn't believe he could be this mean. That he
would laugh at her like this. Tease her and lead her on
and leave her like this.

"He's gone *senile!*" she said, crying this aloud and letting her head thump on the table without mind for how
unseemly or undignified she might be. "Senile," she
groaned, "with no more heart to him than a rake! A dog,
just a hairless cur!" She let her head go on banging
down, wanting to knock this view of him out of her head
and to dispel all view of herself as well. Bile, ugly bile,
stole up her throat and she knew she must spit it out or
ever have it there. Edward Hopkins could do what Ike
not a week ago had said one of his teachers could do. He
could go fuck himself! He could just fuck off. He could
drop dead and fuck off and go screw himself.

"You can do that!" she said, driving herself to the foot of
the stairs and shouting it up to him. *"You can fuck off! You
take the cake when it comes to being a plain asshole!"*

Nothing, only a weighted silence from above—and
something like dots in front of her eyes, dots inflating
and deflating as they sifted down. Her knees gave suddenly out under her and she tumbled back against the
wall. A yellow flower done up in her mama's needlepoint
in a frame on the opposite wall swung on its wire. Somehow, even falling, her eyes went to that. And the picture
went on swinging—at last to float out into space, hang
askew, and be still—all as she herself was slumping
down. Then it seemed to her the whole wall, her whole

sense of hallway and stairs, just broke loose and backed up some. It backed up in a roll and quiver, like sheets of tin hit by heat waves, in that second before it backed off altogether to become an open field, field folding in upon field in another kingdom far from here and sweeter, oh sweeter than her own.

She feels woozy, Ella Mae does. A mite woozy in the head. A touch on the fainty side. Like somebody started a brush fire up there and the wind changed. One stocking has rolled down below her kneecap and she pulls that up. She does, but it takes a while. It seems pulling up a stocking is more than she can manage. Trashy, she thinks, that's what I feel like. Woozy. Oh, I feel woozy. And so trashy-looking with this naked stocking leg. Like that paid woman I used to see sitting on a crate sometimes down at Cal's Store. Feeble, that was her name, on account of her being feeble-minded and showing men everything she had. No, what is the matter with me? Phoebe was that woman's name, a good woman though plain as a stump. That paid woman was another one I was thinking of. Eula, for instance, if ever you catch her out of men's trouser pants.

Finally her stocking is up. It is not up high as she would wish it, but it at least is up. She is decent-looking once more. Feeble. Funny she'd call that woman that. Feeble is what her daddy had called her when he was feeling good and was in a calling mood. After a drink or two and before he turned bad. *You'd be a decent child if you weren't so feeble in the brains.* Well, who was feeble now?

That's what she'd like to ask him. Sitting in a rocking chair day by day, never knowing he had wet himself. Too lazy or stubborn or *feeble* to take himself off to a bathroom. Her stockings might squeeze her legs, they might roll down, but she would never do that. God wouldn't let her. God looked after His own. Like her preacher said, God took care of His pals.

She giggled, then gave a full-blown laugh. Oh, Preacher, she thought, you got off a good one that time. *God and His pals.* You better watch out you don't get hit by lightning bolts. She stayed awhile grinning, reflecting on the makeup of those pals. After the Disciples, after the Prophets, who would He have? Would He have her or Winnameer Riser or Jack Coombs? Would He hold out for the better-known leaders of men? Did He ever say *I'm feeling worn out and beat down today, send in old Mahalia Jackson to sing me a song?* Did He say *I'm in the mood for a good deep throat, send in George Beverly Shea?* Did He ever sometimes just sit down and let somebody preach to *Him? All right, Billy, let's see what you can do. Pull out all your stoppers now!*

She feels woozy, Ella Mae does, but not so woozy as to be willing to go on like this. She is courting suicide by this joking about God, and it is a surprise to her that He has not already sent a messenger to smite her with brickbats and sever off her one healthy hand. But for His love, she supposes, He certainly would. She gropes herself up, grunting and straining, though hardly feeling this as hard work. Hardly feeling anything at all, if truth be known, for she is woozy, a mite touched in the head. It seems to her someone has come along to drop hornets in her mouth, and she doesn't like that either, though she's happy the walls are in place again. She can fix back her mama's picture, for instance, if she wants to. And she wants to, and will. She rights herself and stands leaning against the door, waiting for the swirl to go away and her brains to come back. Who would ever think that mere standing was such a chore? Such a blessing in reverse.

She trudges over and gets her mama's needlepoint back as it was.

"There, Mama," she says, "now you can sleep."

Mama was not much of a one for home crafts, had not the time. So far as she knows, this flower—once bright yellow, now the color of ragweed—is one of the few pieces her mama ever got around to. This flower, and her HOME SWEET HOME over the stove spelled out in broken-up glass. Home *Sweat* Home is what it ought to have been. *Honey, if we hang this about right here or maybe over there by the table, it will sure go a long way to prettify this room.* Later on, with Mama dead, her daddy had wanted to throw it in the fire. *What you want that junk for? If your mama hadn't set around sewing and mending and making junky house things, we might have made something of ourselves. We'd be somebody today.* That being one of her daddy's favorite lines: *Have a drink, Charlie, let's be somebody!*

Oh God, Ella Mae thinks, I've got to get off this one-line track. Got to get myself to a place this train don't stop at. Go somewhere I never been. More food, that is the place my train is going, and anybody don't like it they can just step aside.

"Woo-woo!" she sings, laughing, pumping up and down her good hand, riding the Woozy Express.

It surprises her to find the kitchen lights still on, throwing out a glare painful to her eyes. But why should it surprise me? she asks herself. Did I imagine all my wooziness was to be lived in the dark? This idea is pleasing to her, so she turns the lights off. But the darkness is instantly horrifying to her, since she finds she can't see. She giggles, thinking she has arrived at a triumph of some kind by this discovery, and so turns the lights on once more.

"Oh, giddy," she says, "I feel giddy as a hen."

Her stove clock says half-past ten and she studies it hard, certain that either the clock is wrong or she can't read. But half-past ten is what it says, and this astonishes her. What person in her right mind would be up at this hour, save there wasn't death or sickness in the house? For all she knows, there is. Maybe there is this moment hanging on the front door a wreath with a card stuck to it saying *In deepest sympathy in your time of mourning.* Maybe this minute Jack Coombs is writing in his radio speech *Sympathies of the season for Ella Mae Hopkins and her kith and kin.*

She's tired, she's yawning now. It's high time she called it a night. In a minute, she decides, soon as my stomach has its fill. She goes to the refrigerator and stares in. So much food. So many choices she has. She can see what God has been trying to say to her. *Ella Mae, I made a big mistake with you. I made a mistake with you and with all people of your kind. I made a terrible blunder with the starving people of China and with all those blacks in the Banana Republics. I did it again with the Vietnamese and the Cambodians and with the multitude of refugees tracking all over my land. I did it with all the mobs of humanity who for hatred of their poverty have been wanting since Day One to shoot rather than to kiss my hand. I ought to have stuck with what I knew in the beginning was established fact: forget the Have-nots and stick with the Haves. I spent too much of my time worrying about Jews. Dividing bread to feed five thousand when I should have been hard at work in the mint. Because this much you can take from me: if you don't come to birth with a dollar bill gripped tight in your hand, you are good as kaput. You are good as rubbed out, never mind whether we are talking about the people on Mars or on Earth or those in heaven or hell. All of those people who don't have it I should have wiped out with a plague, and for all of you hardheads who have been scratching to get it I should have tossed in the sponge. You can go*

*ahead and eat now, Ella Mae, for I have had my say. I was done
with your kind long before you were born. You are no more than
dust in my eyes, specks on my sliding board as you slide down.
You've had hell on earth and you can take it from me that only
more of it awaits. I've got plenty of it, my cup runneth over. The
jug of milk that used to cost you ten cents will now cost you a dollar. My admission price has gone up up up until now it is sky-
high, but don't blame me. I have it as my duty to keep ahead of the
times. So eat, Ella Mae. Eat to your heart's content, for it is the
only contentment you will ever get from me.*

Ella Mae's heart is squeezing, thinking these thoughts.
She has put her fingers in her ears to hold away this
voice, though she hears it anyway and is nodding her
head to every word God says. She stands leaning first on
one foot and then on the other, blinking her eyes against
what has appeared to her as a swinging light. She must
have something to hold on to. She must find a chicken
leg or a tree stump and slam it in her mouth. She must
hook herself up to respirator or threshing machine so she
can chew it up fast. Get that little satisfaction down to
her serpent before God goes good on His word and
swoops her up and jams her inside his crowded bag. The
Dairy Queen tub is still on the table and if only to have
the touch of something, she picks up that. Here is where
this started, she remembers, not twenty minutes ago. I
was sitting out in the truck minding my own business,
then I was in here eating and fainting and now minding
His. I ate and got woozy and now I've got wasps in my
mouth and this room is too hocus-pocus for me to sit
down. I'm here turning in a circle, not knowing which
way to turn next. But I do have this bucket in my hand
and I guess I can do what women have always done, I
can wash it up. I can run water and soap it and dry it
and put it away in my pantry with the rest.

She wonders again if Edward has had to pay full price

for what was no good. For what tasted fine but caused all
this giddiness in her. She ought to take this tub to Dairy
Queen, demand her money back. Say to Estelle *This here
tasted okay, but did you drop your nail polish in it? Did your policeman friend leave it to age under his exhaust pipe while the two
of you were rolling on the floor?* Estelle would say *Since you ate
it all in one go, I'm not surprised you got sick. You should have
saved some for tomorrow when you will wish you had. If you're
looking for refunds, you'd best keep on going.* No, you couldn't
expect any satisfaction from a business person, large or
small. You could drop dead for all they cared, so long as
before you dropped you'd taken care to leave all your
money to them. She was glad to know now that if God
was running the place He'd let her have all she wanted.
Eat eat eat, that's exactly what He'd said. Nor did this
surprise her. If it comes down to that, she thinks, you had
to admit food runs through the Holy Book thick as the
avenging sword. There was hardly a page you could
open to that you didn't see written on it words about
breaking bread or dividing up wine. Hardly ever had she
sat down to the Book without a ravenous appetite coming over her. Yes sir, the people in the Book had liked to
fill their stomachs the same as her. As Elijah said to
Ahab, "Get thee up, eat and drink!" It hadn't sailed past
her that the last thing Jesus wanted on earth was a good
supper. He knew Judas Iscariot would betray him, but
he wasn't about to let it spoil his appetite. Whosoever ta-
keth of this sop, Jesus had said, he shall be the one. And
Judas had taken it and they had gone right on eating,
every one of them. The workman, the Lord said, is worthy of his meat. And even with Jesus dead and returning
for a quick visit with his Disciples, the thing uppermost
in his mind was eats. *Have ye here any meat?* Before he'd
said a word about how he'd managed his rising, he'd said
that very thing: *Have ye here any meat?* And he'd sat right

down to broiled fish and a honeycomb, probably not once thinking how fattening that honey would be.

She feels touched in the head. There is a tingling along her scalp and on the back of her neck, and for some minutes she has been scratching at these spots, unaware. Skin burns where her nails have raked flesh, though she gives this no particular acknowledgment either. Self-pity is what she is feeling, and self-pity to her way of thinking is a sorrier sight than a bloated-up dog. It is sorrier by a long shot. She would like to be able this minute to walk like a young hart, to run like a roe, but it has occurred to her that her walking and running days are over. That she will go nowhere after tonight. That she will enter a cave and a rock will be pushed up to the opening. She yawns, her eyelids fall; before her mouth closes on one yawn, her head is already lolling back and her mouth is opening in another. She brings her hands up in front of her face, staring at them, for it seems to her that everything's going numb. Poison. That's what it was. And in her mind's eye she sees Edward and the boys gathered around the table, hee-hawing, poking each other's ribs as they doctor her ice cream, howling like maniacs as they pour the poison in—and then Edward hunching over the table with the purple crayon tight in his hand, thinking to fool her with his words of tender love. They have put poison into her system, no question of that. She could go to the sink now and try to vomit it up, but she won't. Ought to, but won't. They have wanted her to take it, so she will try to keep it down; she will try when her time comes to roll over and kick out her legs and die in such a way as to be the least problem to them. Not a week ago she'd seen Eula Joyner pick up by the scruff of its stiff neck some cat that her dogs had got at, and walk straightaway to her property line and throw it over into the neighbor's yard. Edward could do the same with her.

He could put her in a wheelbarrow and haul her off and leave her to rot in Old Man Rice's cornfield.

Or maybe to murder and be done with her is not what was meant. Maybe a suicide pact has been drawn up and they've assumed what my vote would be. Could be the three of them are upstairs this minute sleeping the sleep of death. Having realized that their lives are as no-account as mine. She could see the headline in tomorrow's paper: YARD MAN RUNS AMOK, KILLS SELF, THEN FAMILY—and see Eula Joyner with her feet up reading it, giving her own explanation to reporters calling by. *I'd say it was brought on by Ella Mae's concern over her weight problem and by them boards over her window and by Edward's worrying about the layoff that looms. And as for the boys, well, they were doing poorly at school, you know, and had these haircuts I wouldn't have put on a bat.* Sensible people reading the news would recognize the deeper truth. They'd say, There but for the grace of God go I, and mean it. They'd say, What it finally came down to was that Edward and Ella Mae and the boys reached the point where their back was to the wall and the only question they knew to ask was What does all our struggling count? What does it avail? What does goodness count—or faith or hope or charity—in a world where wolf attacks wolf and sheep eat off each other and bones are left to rot in open air? A long shadow lay on the soul and it was the absence of any light breaking that done them in.

That was part of it, yes, and it was terrible, but at least it was respectable. It was dignified. Her church preached against it and called it a sin, but that was the whole church talking and not the way members talked when they got home. Between you, me, and the gatepost, they'd say, I've thought about doing the same many a time.

And supposing they weren't dead. She could go upstairs and drive a stake through each heart, and God wouldn't lift a finger. He wouldn't twitch an eye. He wouldn't, and that was wrong. It was wrong of her to do it and wrong of God to let it be done, and the only reason it was done was that there was no God. It was high time she faced up to the truth, and that was the one truth facing her now. God was pie in the sky if he was anything at all.

She moves to turn off the light, moves at long last to bolt the door. She wheels and runs, plunging in a trot through the darkness of the house, forcing a wide path for herself as she drives upstairs toward her bedroom, where she can't wait to throw down her head and die. To get it over with.

Yet the stairs are so steep! They are so rubbery, and folding under her. It seems to her that nothing made by man should be so hard to climb, or that this darkness in which she moves should be so thick, so deep and full, so terrifying. The thought comes to her that somehow without her knowledge she has already passed over to the other side, that this is the fateful darkness one plunges through after God's back has turned and Satan's quick hand is the only hand left you can grab. She weeps, she can hear herself weeping now, crying in horrible fear, wanting to claim mistakes have been made, that she should be on another road, on God's road if only for another little while, but not letting herself screech such madness out, admitting to herself that what mistakes have been made have been made by her alone and it is up to her now to put them right. Even so, to follow the black pitch of this road is more than she can manage, and while it is shabby of her to expect help, she understands that help is what she must have and that there is no one she can call to for that except Edward. And so the next moment she is screaming, hands pressed against her ears that this abominable weakness may be less painful to her or even that she may pretend this screeching is erupting from the mouth of some woman not known to her—*Edward, help me, help me—Edward oh Edward help me now!*

Lights flash on, dim, then brighten and stay on, swinging to and fro as if they hang one behind the other on a string. The boys are at their doorway, naked but for their boxer shorts, rubbing their eyes, while Edward has materialized under her right arm to say *There, there, lean on me, don't you worry your pretty head one iota.* To lead her along, saying *Old Doctor Edward is here, he will see you through all misery, bring you roaring back into beautiful health, into warmth and sunshine.* To wipe her wet eyes and stroke her cheeks with the back of his hand and murmur *Sit down here, old gal, stretch out and relax, I'll take off these shoes, get you out of that sticky dress.* To sink and stretch down beside her, his voice gone soft and climbing over her like ivy over a rain barrel, *Rest easy now, sweetheart, close your eyes. Forget all your worries about window or weight, about what is boarded up, for you know what I have done I have done for your own good. Be morning before you know it, old darling, a good night's rest and you'll be springing back on us good as new. Old Doctor Edward is ready and able, you can give yourself up to him.* To hold her and to say these words and to vanish as he is patting bedcovers to her neck, shifting pillow under her head, saying, *Sleep, Ella Mae, sleep, my darling, that's the honey, that's my sweet little girl* . . .

Butter on butter and every dab of it smooth.

"There, there," he whispers. "Sweet dreams, my love."

Breath on breath and every heave of it good.

She can see all the way back through to where it is she has come to this place from. She can clench and unclench her eyes and hold her breath and think to herself *Where I am is not bad. No, it is not half-bad. I am in my own bed and Edward is beside me and what else could I ask for?*

Nothing. There is nothing else she could ask for.

"Just sleep, my love. Saw your logs and dream your dreams."

Oh, I will. I will saw my logs and dream my dreams, knowing I am safe here. I am at peace and can know my heart's rest here.

Yet a sob escapes her, even so—as Edward fits his body against hers, as his head snuggles up under the hollow of her chin, as his hand comes to warm rest over her stomach's high curve. She blinks her eyes and holds him close, sobbing anew, for the darkness is unyielding, it is merciless and uncaring and black as pitch and it gives nothing back. Nothing, not even the sweep of her hand. A chill steals over her. She lifts her sore finger and looks at it but nothing is there. Only the pain is.

"Edward?"

Edward yawns. She can hear his breath smoothing out, his body relaxing into sleep. Slipping away. She tightens her hold on him, pressing his head down on her.

"Don't do it," she murmurs. "Don't fall asleep on me yet." Her voice is ragged and harsh and not as she means it to be. She would say *please* but has not the strength. She would beg and entreat, but her eyes are heavy, she has not the strength. She trembles, staring up into the dark. It seems to her that this darkness is all-knowing and all-powerful, that it is a darkness swirled up out of time long past, out of some silent emptiness that existed long before the world was made, come now by Edward's bidding to claim her with its dampness and rot.

She looks, whimpering, to where her window would

be, to the door where that would be. "Edward," she asks, "what do you aim to do with me?"

He twitches. He is awake and listening to her. A bony knee flies up and leaves its bruise on her.

"You mean to hide me off up here? You mean to seal me away forever?"

"Not forever, Ella Mae."

"How long then?"

"Nothing else has worked, Ella Mae. You have gone on getting bigger and bigger, a trial to yourself and us. All I mean to do is whittle you down, get you back to fighting size." He buries a kiss in her hot neck. "It won't be no picnic, my darling, but you got to remember I am only doing it for your own good."

Her hands are up covering her ears.

"I got the doctor coming by to saw off that ring, and if you don't let him, I mean to take my wire cutters to it. At daybreak I'm putting in a little cat door so I can slide in enough food to keep you going. I'll ask Eula to come over and pass the time of day with you. She can stand outside in the grass and you two can jaw about whatever you want to. Me and the boys have checked it out, you can hear everything fine through the boards. You'll live Ella Mae. You'll thank me for it one day."

He wouldn't do this to someone he loves. No, he might do this to skunk or polecat, but he couldn't do this to her.

"You'll see. Just trust me."

She does not know where her voice has got to. Where her pride has gone or why all her wits should desert her now. She should be leaping from the bed, tearing away this minute and shrieking his name up and down the street, telling the world how evil her Edward has become. Should, but she hasn't the strength. She cannot move. She cannot rise up and struggle against darkness heavy as this.

"I'd rather be dead," she moans.

He snuggles close as he can. His hand slides on down over her stomach. It smooths out her wiry hair there and pushes on down between her legs.

"I would, Edward."

She grinds her eyes shut, but lets him put the part in her legs. She opens her legs for him. She would make a space where even this darkness might thrive. She would make her wide flesh be everything, a lake of cream to drown in, a field of earth in which Ella Mae Hopkins and everybody like her, all the world's poor and miserable, might forever cuddle—cuddle and hide.

Oh hide me, she thinks.

"Feel good?" he says.

A NOTE ON THE TYPE

This book was set, via computer-driven cathode-ray
tube, in a film version of a typeface called Baskerville.
The face itself is a facsimile reproduction of types cast
from molds made for John Baskerville (1706–75) from
his designs. Baskerville's original face was one of the
forerunners of the type style known as "modern face"
to printers—a "modern" of the period A.D. 1800.

Composed by American Book–Stratford Press,
Saddle Brook, New Jersey
Printed and bound by the Haddon Craftsmen,
Scranton, Pennsylvania

Book design by Judith Henry